# SPENT LIGHT

# Spent Light

A BOOK

Lara Pawson

CB *editions*

First published in the UK in 2024
by CB editions
146 Percy Road London W12 9QL
www.cbeditions.com

All rights reserved

© Lara Pawson, 2024

Lines from *White Egrets* by Derek Walcott reprinted
by permission of Faber and Faber Ltd.
Lines from 'Correctives' from *Rain* by Don Paterson. Published by
Faber & Faber Ltd., 2009. Copyright © Don Paterson. Reproduced
by permission of the author c/o Rogers, Coleridge & White Ltd.,
20 Powis Mews, London W11 1JN.

The right of Lara Pawson to be identified as author of this work
has been asserted in accordance with the Copyright,
Designs and Patents Act, 1988

Printed in England by Imprint Digital, Exeter

ISBN 978-1-7394212-2-9

For Perk

I have nothing in common with experimentalists, adventurers, with those who travel to strange regions. The surest, and the quickest, way for us to arouse the sense of wonder is to stare, unafraid, at a single object.

Cesare Pavese, *Dialogues with Leucò*, 1947


And the crack in the tea-cup opens
A lane to the land of the dead.

W. H. Auden, 'As I Walked Out One Evening', 1940

When I think back to how we first met, Reg is standing, smiling, in a woollen coat in winter and I am in shorts, my bare legs enjoying the heat of the sun. When I zoom in on the memory of that moment, Reg fills the screen. His stainless-steel spectacles, his combed-over hair, and his brown Derby shoes laced up tight. I slip out of shot.

I couldn't say the two of us ever managed to close the gap and become friends, but warmth was there from the start.

More often than not, when I was popping to the shops or on my way back home, Reg would call out from his front door and we would engage in light conversation. Our relationship grew like this for several years. Layer upon layer of chat about holidays, the weather, our neighbours, local politics, vegetables, World War II, and cars. I learned that he'd always voted Conservative and that he still went ballroom dancing, alone, every Wednesday night.

He rarely spoke about his wife, whose name I recall as Jean. The name Jean may be on my mind because an academic, whose work I like, is called Jean, and her partner, also an academic, whose work I also like, or used to like more than I do now, has been mentioned a lot on social media because he has been accused of sexually harassing his students.

Whatever her name was, I never actually saw Reg's wife, not even a hand behind the nets behind their clean, closed windows. There were days when I doubted she existed at all. Days when he said he'd taken her to the doctor and he'd gesture at the car, but the car was always empty and cold. It was during one of these exchanges that I learned they'd never married but had lived together since the 1950s in the same terraced house halfway up our street.

When the stairlift appeared in the front garden, I knew she was dead. Reg came rushing out of the house and pushed a toaster into my hands. I've a better one in Chingford anyway, he said.

I remember looking up to the sky. The starched light of the sun was pushing through the clouds. I was straining to keep my eyes open, trying to see what was inside the blinding white haze.

I thanked him and strode home, the plug bouncing off my leg, your semen still leaking into the gusset of my pants.

I had never owned a toaster before.

It has good dimensions. Like those leather handbags that used to be held at the elbow by women of a certain leaning, women who lent their husbands their garters and attended funerals in pillbox hats.

At one end, three buttons the shape of pellets of rat shit. Above each button, a shell of red plastic encases a tiny bulb. If I rub one of these for a moment or two, the dog's nipple comes to mind, or the trigger pin on an Arma-Lite semi-automatic, or that inarticulate surge of pleasure when your finger closes in on my clitoris.

Above each light, fractionally off centre, a word is printed in the same restrained font found in CIA documents. Together, they form a synopsis of the anthropocene: REHEAT DEFROST CANCEL.

To the right of these buttons is a dial the size of an adult anal sphincter. It has a dorsal fin that is the most elegant aspect of the entire machine, sparking visions of a porpoise curling in and out of breaking waves. It is the most sinister, too. Not because the porpoise died with twenty-three plastic bags in its stomach and the string from a tampon of a girl who panicked and ran to the sea to secrete this foreign object the only way she knew how, but because the dial controls heat.

Heat, like a sharp rise on the price of bread, can trigger strife. Indeed, in Egypt, bread is known as aysh, which is Arabic for life.

The whole thing is encased in steel stained on one side with the paw prints of a startled cat. It has a skirt, too. A thick black skirt that hides the machine's feet and the intricate connections that convert electricity into heat. A skirt that turns my thoughts to that old woman who sat across the aisle from us on the bus to Órgiva.

As the long vehicle swept in and out along the twisting road of the Alpujarra, she began to sweat, her hands to fuss, and bile and bits of breakfast congregated between her lips. Then her eyes became wet, she said she couldn't breathe through her nose, and she held that long white envelope like a cradle to her mouth.

It was only after the final turn into the town that the tension eased. She spread her feet and, from beneath her long black skirt, panting in the heat, the tongue of a solid old dog.

She said she was six when a bullfighter called Pepe pointed a gun at her mother and gave the order to drink from a bottle of castor oil. Aggressive vomiting was followed by rapid labour, the little girl watching as the knot of wet flesh flopped on to the parched street of the beautiful hilltop town. She said she still remembered the smell of her mother's diarrhoea and the silence that came down like heavy velvet when the brick sunk into her brother's soft skull.

Because I think of that woman whenever I use the toaster,

and because I think of her mother being forced to drink castor oil, sometimes I imagine myself being forced to drink it, too. Sometimes I even imagine myself forcing someone else to drink it.

What would have had to happen to me to make me be so cruel?

When I asked you if you knew that castor beans contain ricin, you said you had no idea. I showed you a picture from the internet to try to convince you of their allure. I did not tell you that I'd already taken certain steps towards acquiring some for myself. Just a handful to pour from one palm to the other to take stock of the beauty of poison.

Their glossy beetle backs would sit well inside the ashtray that was blown to a bowl, like a curled kilo of Golden Syrup, somewhere in Scandinavia. How I admire the weight of that glass! And to think of all those forgotten years since it held your father's ash when he was working late, pushing his pencil along the stainless-steel ruler his aunt gave him in 1949.

The pipe you remember most fondly was made from clay cooked to a yellowy grey with folds that formed the face of a man with a beard and a jaunty hat. A jolly wayfarer, you said with uncharacteristic hesitation, and probably

German. The next word you spoke was Meerschaum, which excited me so much I asked you to repeat it.

The skin on your face softened as you recalled your father's trips to the tobacconist, a tiny old shop in the middle of town. He'd return home with four pouches, each holding a different leaf from a different part of the world. You were tasked with shredding the leaves into a single pile on the coffee table, which had been placed in the lounge as an expression of an ambition for dinner parties. Though I don't think they ever had a single one, you said with a flatness that felt deserved.

Kneeling bare-legged on the shag-pile rug, which was as foamy as waves crashing into Cornish cliffs, you took care to tear one leaf from each pouch in turn so that the final mix would be balanced and pleasing to your father's taste. As your fingers worked the dried brown matter – which, from the way you described it, looked a little like the dried fish stacked on trays balanced on the heads of women beside Lake Volta – you would lift the occasional piece to your nose and inhale the aroma, rousing in your imagination a vision of a field far away where a boy was briskly pulling at bushes and throwing into the basket on his back the same leaves you held in your unblemished hands in the Mersey burbs.

Some days you wished you were that boy. Others, you were an astronaut.

It was your friend who gave us the pepper mill. The composer. The one who wrote that astonishing opera about the serial-killing necrophiliac. The pepper mill belonged to his father, who'd worked as a waiter at The Ritz for years. He came to London in 1958 from a town tucked into the hem of the Lattari mountains. The composer's grandfather was a cobbler who walked to work across a valley of flowers and black snakes. When the composer took us there, you stepped on one of the snakes as you ran down some stone steps and I watched it whip your foot with its tail.

The three of us went on a long walk, following steep paths into the hills, higher and higher, until we were wading through bracken that fingered our throats. We were followed by a patrol of mountain dogs, their camouflage coats so matted with mud we hadn't noticed them guarding their sheep. Then the clouds came down and it began to rain and we pretended to each other that the way was always forward, but the paths we chose kept disappearing, one after the other, eroded into air.

When we could no longer hide the panic behind our eyes, we became horribly afraid and ever more lost. You took my hand and you held it hot and hard.

The pepper mill feels like a hand grenade made to fit my fist. Its wooden body bulges in the middle and, from the centre of its brass lid, an elegant handle like a safety lever reaches out to the side. Instead of pulling the pin and flipping it up, you turn the wooden knob clockwise between finger and thumb, grinding down the peppercorns inside.

The brass top has a hatch the size of a frog's kidney. To open it, you tuck a fingernail against the brass nipple and slide it anti-clockwise. To fill the mill, you pour peppercorns through this hole into the dark.

I can't look at it without seeing myself throwing it from the upstairs window at a man striding up the street with an RPG and a knife. I always see a cat, too. At the side of the road, it is writhing in pain.

I wish I'd known, when I was still a child, that the term hand grenade comes from the Spanish for pomegranate, which is rooted in the Latin, granatus, which means full of seeds.

Has anyone ever managed to grind peppercorns into the eyes of a rapist down a dark alley, as I was advised? How much more appealing to greet him with a hand grenade that has been tested on six-millimetre plywood. The sort of grenade that can blow off limbs or blow out lungs or blow out a musician's ear drum. A lightweight model would do, one that weighs a little over six ounces.

Our pepper mill weighs five, whereas a good Italian lemon weighs eight. I know this because, following the waiter's death, I took care of his lemon tree.

Its highest leaf was level with my hips, and buxom lemons hung from branches that were thin but strong. Its roots were contained in a turquoise pot, broad like the backside of the peasant riding his mule into those fearless Italian hills. He sat on the animal as if it were a bench, his legs not astride but hanging down one side, his heels rubbing its ribs. He was holding a brown bottle in one hand and supporting the side of his head with the other. There was a lot of sweat. There was the rhythm of the mule.

I'm watching steam rising from the eggs. I turn the grinder and here I am following your composer again.

At the start of the summer holidays, when he was still a boy, his mother would write the address of his father's family onto a piece of card and tie it with gardening string to the front of his coat. She made her son four sets of sandwiches and wrapped waxed paper around a slice of marble cake. She put money into a purse, which she would push into his pocket once they'd reached Victoria Station.

One year, as she ran alongside the train, smiling and flushed, waving at her little boy at the start of his journey all the way down to Naples, she felt in her own pocket the small suede purse.

It was lunchtime when he reached the Gare du Nord. He imagined a tapeworm bellowing into the tannoy as he stepped onto the concourse. Without money he could not buy the ticket to take him to the Gare de Lyon, so he chose a pillar and stood firmly beside it, watching and wondering and waiting.

He was considering unwrapping the cake when he was approached by a tall, trembling man. They exchanged several words and the man bent over the child and reached for his hand. When the boy felt the man's fingers fluttering in his palm, his thoughts switched to the moth he had caught before Easter when he was hiding in his father's garden shed. He held the man's hand as delicately as he could, taking care not to grip too tight with his own.

It was not clear, as they left the station, who was leading whom, nor why they took such short steps.

Together, they walked down Paris streets the boy had never seen before. They passed cafés and statues, and the boy was impressed by all the pigeons and slender women and the men holding guns. He understood Danish and spoke good Italian. He had enough French to ask the basics. By the time they reached the Gare de Lyon, he knew that the man spoke a language called Wolof, that he'd lived in Paris for twelve years, that he was nearly fifty-three.

On the platform, the man's arms were wobbling so much that his elbow started flapping like a flag against his ribs and he struggled to reach inside his jacket. When the dark slender fingers reappeared, they held five quivering notes. The boy took the money and tucked it into a sock. He blushed.

The following morning, he was with his grandmother at the market outside Naples. Pick yourself one of these, she said, and I'll be back. He looked at the stack of wooden cages holding chickens and ducks and rabbits and geese. When the old woman returned, he pointed at a rabbit with a blue eye.

For the next six weeks, he took great care of the soft, pillowy animal. He fattened and watered it. He cleaned out its hutch. In the mornings, before it was too hot, he let it roam free. He followed it as it hopped about, keeping an eye on the piece of string he had taken from his coat and tied to the rabbit's hind leg.

The day before he returned to London, the boy's grandmother called him to the kitchen and held his body close to her side. She gripped his shoulder with her cold, wide fingers. Now you need to break its neck, she said, like this.

There is a squirrel's tail in a jam jar on the shelf inside the top door of the fridge-freezer, which is the smallest two-door fridge-freezer in the world according to the man with the kind face who sold it to me. I still don't know how to interpret his claim, but that middle-aged woman from Kent – the one you invited for lunch in the summer, who'd damaged her hip picking up a box of Bran Flakes with her teeth – well, she compared this particular white good to a hotel mini-bar while boasting that her cocaine habit had absolutely no bearing on the deaths of children in Colombia. As to the tail, it belonged to the first grey squirrel I ever skinned.

Initially, I thought about selling it to the Canadian who makes flies for fly-fishing, but he only buys them in bundles of fifty. So I came up with the more ambitious plan to turn it into a keyring for one of my godchildren – a lucky charm, I suppose – which led to a brief but intense addiction to YouTube videos made entirely by white North American men, mostly in combat gear, standing beside a rifle and a pile of dead squirrels and a pick-up truck in the middle of a forest somewhere in the Deep South.

My favourite was from West Virginia. It begins high in the branches of an old mulberry tree. A slightly cross-eyed man with a true red neck and a polar-bear tattoo on his deltoid is chucking mulberries down his throat while merrily articulating the delights of this fruit. In the next shot, he's on the ground, standing in front of some shagbark hickory trees. A grey squirrel hangs lifeless in his hand. Straight up he admits he did not kill it. His daughter did. She popped it off, he tells us proudly, with this nice twenty-two.

He is the one who will be skinning it, however – and he

does so with a fluency and efficiency that stirs feelings inside me of greatness and beauty. With an elegant blade, he makes a slice at the very base of the tail, right up tight to the anus. He cuts through the bone, but takes care not to break the skin and fur on the other side. He places the squirrel onto its back on the ground and stands firm on its tail. Holding the hind legs in one hand, he pulls up hard and the skin comes clean off, stripping the dead animal naked, all the way up to its neck.

The first time I watched this, I was overcome with the memory of my grandmother telling me to raise my arms up in the air so she could pull my jumper over my head to undress me to go to bed.

The other night, when you came to bed, you were pulling my pyjama top over my head when you hesitated at the very moment that my face was smothered in blue brushed cotton and my arms trapped inside the buttoned-up body above me. My eyes were closed. I contained the panic, swallowing the sudden conviction that you were going to leave me there to suffocate.

That first squirrel! Its meat was so sweet. I wondered if I'd pinched at the sugar, not the salt. I think you'd swallowed only two mouthfuls when you put down your bowl and ran upstairs to the bathroom. From the sofa, I listened to your retching and groaning.

Is this psychological? I shouted.

Your answer was a long silence. Then I heard the loo seat bounce and the flush of water and you appeared at the top of the stairs, a sleeve across your mouth.

All those tiny bones, you said, like a fish.

Yet you returned to your chair and lifted the bowl from the floor, placed it on your lap, and proceeded to eat most of what remained of the casserole with the carrots and onions, the garlic, a few twigs of thyme, and at least a pint of homemade chicken stock. With wet fingers, you passed me the ribcage and the dog stared as I plucked at the meat with my sharpest front teeth.

In fact, that was his fourth squirrel, but his sixth kill. The other two were rats, one of which he caught in the dark when he was standing beside me on the edge of the pond where that woman's body was found chopped up inside an IKEA bag. I remember the rat's screams slicing through the night. I remember hearing men fucking in a bush.

I have often thought I would definitely eat rat if I was trapped in a famine, and have sometimes wondered whether I would eat a human if, for example, I had survived a plane crash in the middle of nowhere and was losing hope of being rescued any time soon. If I did, would I compare the taste and texture of human flesh to that of a sheep or a pig or a cow?

Whenever I tell anyone I've eaten squirrel, they always want to know what it tastes like. Is it like rabbit? Or chicken? Or more like venison? I've been surprised by the number of people who claim to remember the taste of rabbit.

More curious is that it never occurred to me, in those moments when I was considering surviving on humans and rats, that I might, one day, eat a squirrel – and do so for pleasure. It was only when the dog had caught and killed three that the idea of a meal entered my mind.

The first stayed where he dropped it, by the path running through the Victorian filter beds, close to where we launched the Chinese paper balloon to celebrate the life of our dead friend. The second, he left on the edge of the towpath, and the third beneath some trees beside a football pitch. When I looked back, all I could see was a soft toy, dropped from the hand of the child slumped in the pushchair.

Now, I always walk with a rucksack and a plastic bag. I've invested fifteen pounds in a Whitby Wild Cat skinning knife, which I bought from a man with a skin condition in a specialist hunting shop in a town in the south. He told me that his brother skins squirrels too – Shoots the buggers with an air rifle! – and that he swears by the Wild Cat.

The blade is short and sharp and bevelled on both sides. It has a gut hook that looks like a hawk's beak if you point the tip of the knife to the sky. It is this hook that brings on

Hannibal Lecter – that shivery sucking – and he's gutting a man alive.

I keep the knife in the right-hand drawer of my desk because I like to admire it when I sit here. Its weight and shape inspire me. Its purpose absolute.

The other day, I spread a copy of the *Financial Times* over the bread board. I lay a grey squirrel carefully on top of the front page, its black whiskers curling over a headline, Policies for a pandemic.

Hours earlier, it had been running with its life from my dog through the woods. He doesn't get them all, but this one he took in his teeth and he shook and he swung, slamming its body around his nose, hurling it against the sides of his head. Even so, the kill was not quick. The squirrel lay on its back, stretchered on wet brown leaves. I counted four gasps for breath and looked with amazement at its tongue. Then it rolled on to its side, curling its nose into its tail, still panting and frail.

There followed some sort of spasm. It stretched back onto its back, its forelegs frantically paddling the air in a final attempt to run back to life. Its glossy black eyes were still wide open when I held a finger to its ribs to check for death before lifting it by its tail and lowering it, headfirst, into my sack.

Back home, in the kitchen, I ran my little finger over its fur. It was still warm, but stiffening. Removing my knife from its canvas sheath, I noticed in myself a certain shift. The squirrel had become an inanimate object that required immediate preparation. I approached it as I might a cauliflower wrapped in coarse leaves – emphatic, without life.

I pinched on the white fluff of what had been its adorable tummy and, with the tip of the blade of my Whitby Wild Cat, poked hard and harder until I felt the pop of the skin giving way. With some excitement, and the help of my curved nail scissors, which I keep in an old Colman's mustard-powder pot behind the bathroom door, I was cutting and slicing, pushing fingers deep inside, tearing silver pelt from purple flesh. I hacked into the top of the tailbone, I sawed through its neck, and I pressed my blade down hard on the delicate bones above each of its feet.

When I noticed that its eyes had closed, I wondered when and how that had happened given that it was, so I had thought, long dead. I felt a twang of guilt at the possibility that, out there in the woods, I had dropped it by its tail into my orange Sainsbury's bag when it was, in fact, still alive. It was the thought that it had known what I was doing – that I had been witnessed – that I did not like. But I did not mind at all that its wet intestines were squeezing between my fingers, leaking into the crevices between cuticle and nail.

I felt no shame or dizziness at the sight of these little

organs and the deep red blood – at the contrast between furry exterior and slippery innards. Skinning this squirrel confirmed my admiration for my dog, and seemed to fertilise my anticipation for the meat I was shortly to eat.

I dropped its skin into the plastic compost bin just as I might a banana's, except I've never paused to glance at the skin of the fruit as I did the emptied face of this soft grey thing now resting on coffee grains and garlic skin, carrot peel, egg shells, rejected porridge and that sorry bloom of flowers that spent too much of its early life inside a refrigerated lorry before finally unfurling in the heavy glass jug we were given by that couple we no longer like.

When you came home, you listened to my account of the day's hunting and you described my attitude to the squirrel as the perfect riposte to transubstantiation. I was so winded by this that the following morning I called on a friend – a proper Catholic, not a lapsed one like you – and I asked her if she really believed that a wafer and a cup of wine could be the flesh and blood of Christ.

I do, she said, and I envied her certainty.

Isn't that a form of cannibalism? I said.

She laughed. She told me about a conversation she'd had with a priest, some years back. He had advised her to think through transubstantiation with bullets.

Whereas Anglicans are content to fire blanks, he'd explained, Catholics use live ammunition.

I've brought other things back from the woods. At the top of a hill, where the land sinks to a basin of stewed water glistening black in the embrace of dead leaves and fallen branches, I found a pile of watermelon skins and a cymbal on a stand.

I studied the scene from behind a hornbeam, its catkins hanging in clusters like the pointless fingers of a stillborn. I was looking for a camera, for wires to a mic. I was scanning the trunks of the trees for the arms of a man. I trained my ears for heavy feet and deep breaths, but nothing cut through the breeze and the rain on the trees except the whipped revs of an engine riding tight to the tarmac somewhere close, somewhere steep. I was hoping for the arrival of a single brown deer, but instead had a vision of a woman attacking her labia with pinking shears. I turned and walked back down the hill into the heart of the forest.

Two days later, I decided to return. It was still raining and the instrument was still there, standing on the same spot beside the silver birch. The watermelon looked even fresher despite remaining untouched. Now, there were clumps of cut celery sprouting lime green leaves.

I approached the cymbal and lent it my ear, but the sound of raindrops hitting bronze seemed unimportant out here. I loosened the screw attaching the stand to three legs and lifted the whole thing by its long, thin neck. Inspired, I swivelled my own body and walked quickly away.

As I crossed the gravel path that leads to the church, I encountered a man. He was leaning on a motorbike watching me. He raised an arm and then his voice: Make a sale, girl! I held his gaze but kept walking. When I looked back I noticed the words Boere Biker stitched to his shoulder blades in ice-cream leather.

Like the lucky bird dropping that streaks the top pocket of my waterproof jacket, and the spots of faeces that the cat sprayed from her anal gland casting a constellation of dark stars across our fitted white sheet, the cymbal is splattered with the mud and rain of the forest and coated in the dust of the house. Here, in my room, I keep it close to my chair so I can tap it with the nail of my right index finger and count the seconds inside the vibrations like the seconds between the launch of an artillery shell and its explosion on landing.

When the dog barks, this slanting circumference of bronze replies with flurries of glittered sound that seem to insist on the existence of something primordial. Often, these moments are interrupted by a vision of Yul Brynner, bald and polished and, let me say it, exotic. Those silk pantaloons!

In 1978, the year I began watching *The Magnificent Seven*, he became the honorary president of the World Roma Congress, an international gathering demanding an end to their discrimination, and an end to the term 'gypsy'. In several obituaries, Brynner's mother is described as a Romanian gypsy bride.

I gave up my bed to a Romanian woman. She gave me a tight crocheted top. It was black and see-through. She said it was sexy and I loathed it. For a long time, it sustained the idea of Romania as a country full of women with pert nipples poking through holes. I was in my twenties. I threw it into the fire on the roof of that house across the green from MI6.

In those days, I pitied people who surrounded themselves with things they owned. I looked down upon those who cherished certain objects so deeply, they found it hard to leave them behind. In order to be free, so I told myself, I would overcome irrational attachment. I would get rid of the things I'd acquired. I would train myself to dislike these belongings that were holding me back, seducing me with their presence.

I gave many away, but some proved resistant – the things that had burrowed into me, like the tick that found the small of my neck where my hair is thick and warm and wet with sweat – so I burned them.

D ecades gone and I still take pleasure from the magnets on my fridge. Even the cooking timer, its blue plastic casing filthy with splashes of milk and whisked egg, pomegranate syrup, prawn stock, vegetable oil and burned sugar, and its plate of barium ferrite – its mucus and muscle – boasting flour and bread crumbs and leaking something sticky.

I love to take it and turn it and hold it to my head, its urgent tick-tick like the carriage clock above the fireplace in that ancient house that always seemed so far away. Low ceilings held up for centuries by the same dark beams.

I wish I could take you back to meet the old man snoring in his upright armchair. Thinking about him now, I see his narrow moustache, his toad trousers and the tank top knitted by his wife. I suppose she'd always expected it. His brown leather shoes still laced with discipline, his hair clipped close and flattened with pomade, his fingers sliding apart on a belly that heaved with the trouble of life.

> And suddenly I saw that there was no afterwards.
> There was no future; nothing further to think.
> There was the war – and that was all –
> curving over me like a wall reaching to the sky,
> limitless, without loophole or chink.
> I could batter my head against that.

So who am I to make the link to the Memopark timer? They were popular in the 1970s. Handy keyring gadgets that had an alarm bell to remind motorists that their parking meter was about to run out. It was while I was watching a documentary about The Troubles that I noticed their resemblance to my magnetic kitchen timer. A priest was boasting about how he'd worked out that these little tools could solve a problem for the IRA, whose bombers kept being blown up by their own devices: It was foolproof! Even if he tried, he couldn't kill himself planting a bomb! They were used in the Warrenpoint attack in 1979, the Hyde Park bombing in 1982, and the Brighton bombing in 1984.

Thirty-four deaths, and all I can think about is the similarity between the blue Memopark timer they showed on the telly and the one slapped to the top door of my fridge-freezer. I long to wind it up and fix it to the underside of our neighbour's car, just to feel it suck to the metal, just to listen to the sound of the tick-tick down there, just to get a taste of what it is to create fear.

Two eggs in a pan of bubbling water – one for you, one for me – and the timer keeps ticking. While I am waiting I'm watching Carol Vorderman, her cheekbones pushing through the TV screen. A violet blouse flows over her body. I reach forward to dip my fingers into the silk, but she raises a finger!

Behind her, a desk. Behind the desk, side by side, a boy

and a man are bent over pieces of paper, scrambling to calculate a single number from six more. Carol tells them they have thirty seconds. At fifteen, the ticking crescendoes accompanied by rapid drumming that accumulates inside a short horn section during which the boy lays down his pencil and looks up. When the timer stops, I bang the lid of the egg pan with my spurtle. The man is still scribbling when the reverberations of the Countdown clock send my thoughts plummeting to a book that won't let go of my head.

Its cover is the pale grey of a gravestone. It has a grainy texture that feels like the surface of a large green leaf. When I lift it, the sensation on my skin seems to trick my fingers into believing that nature is resting upon them. Perhaps that is why I can hold in my hands, night after night, this thing that is overflowing with the minutiae of industrial murder.

In 1943, the killing facilities at Auschwitz Birkenau were upgraded. Crematoria IV and V became a production line of death. Replacing the previous, much more time-consuming process, in which people and bodies were transported between different floors and different areas of the camp, these two buildings held all the necessary facilities on a single level.

Prisoners were ordered to undress. They were sent into a room, which they had been told was a shower but was really a sealed chamber. Precise quantities of Zyklon

Bläusaure crystals were poured through a hole in the roof. The prisoners' lives ended between twenty and thirty minutes later. Their bodies were transferred to large ovens. The man in charge of these killing plants, one Karl Bischoff, said that up to 4,416 bodies were burned every twenty-four hours. The real figure may well have been double that. But even if it wasn't, at least one body was burned every twenty seconds.

I set my kitchen timer to one minute. I make myself imagine three friends being gassed to death and burned to ash.

I set the timer to ten minutes – the amount of time you told me to leave an egg standing in boiled water if I want it hard-boiled to perfection – and I do it again, this time with thirty people I know. I write their names in pencil on a sheet of paper so that I can rub them out later, so no one has to know what I've done and I can pretend to forget.

Your name keeps coming to mind, but I cannot bear to include it.

I can't forget the names of the people killed by Bischoff and his little team because I do not know their names. But I know his, which begs the question: should I be using it, or erasing it?

And I will keep wondering: did he use a timer or did he wait for silence?

I'll never forget the first time the dog caught a muntjac. I wanted to deafen my ears to the animal's screams. I was hiding in the bushes behind an abundance of brambles. I was waiting for the noise to stop.

I had always assumed that the gas chambers were the Nazis' preferred method of killing because they offered the quickest way to end human life on a massive scale. In fact, the largest number of Jews ever killed in a single massacre during the Holocaust took place near Kyiv in Babi Yar at the end of September 1941. In two days, German forces shot 33,711 people dead. I have tried and I have tried but I still can't imagine what that number of human beings looks like. Perhaps that isn't the point.

Because the killers watched their victims fall, sometimes exchanging glances with them as they went down, many were left traumatised.

The appeal of the gas chamber was that it spared the killer.

For years, a postcard was held to the fridge-freezer by the kitchen timer. A nephew and niece sent it from Amsterdam: We think you will really like this! It was a photograph of a woman's face, her lips formed from a pouting anus, her nose from fleshy vulva and labia, her eyes were real eyes but they had been Photoshopped to either side of her clitoral hood. Everything was waxed.

Not a single hair remained, not a trace of any stubble.

It had been there so long, I rarely noticed it. Until one morning when I spotted a brown streak down the side of her face. A line of diarrhoea, I thought, as I put on my reading glasses and knelt down in front of the fridge. While I waited for the kettle to boil, I examined the streak as closely as I could. I realised it was the skin that had formed on the top of my hot chocolate. It must have slipped from the tip of my finger. But the idea of diarrhoea would not disappear. So I tore the card in two. I threw it away.

Looking at the fridge door this morning, at the white space left behind, I'm remembering my vinyl collection. Before we went to Nouakchott, I sold it all to a man named Goose. He had copper-coloured hair and he paid a fair price. But the depth of regret for my records might be equal to the emptiness I touch each time I think of the friendship I found out there. She was Moroccan, as direct as a drill, with breathful beauty.

In an email some years later, I made a mistake and she never replied. We no longer speak. But the conversations we shared have tunnelled deep inside me. I would lie on my back on the thin rug of her office floor watching the fan spinning above. Down there, on the ground, where the air was cool, I remember watching her walk to the window to recite General Franco:

My years in Africa live with me with indescribable force. There, was born the possibility of rescuing a great Spain. There, was founded the idea which today redeems us. Without Africa, I can scarcely explain myself to myself, nor can I explain myself properly to my comrades in arms.

I sensed her irritation when I confessed that I did not know about Franco's years in Morocco. So I promised I would not forget. He was sent there, as a junior officer, in 1912 when it was still a Spanish protectorate. He rose up the ranks to second-in-command of the Spanish Foreign Legion, which carried out the most appalling atrocities in many Moorish villages. Severed heads were put on show. By the time he became Brigadier General in 1928, he was a master of violence and terror and, when he returned home a few years later, he began persecuting Spanish citizens on Spanish soil just as he had the colonial subject in Morocco. His fascist supporters called landless Spanish labourers Berbers and savages. In Andalusia, under Franco's orders, civilians were mutilated, murdered and raped.

It was because of her that I finally understood that the violence meted out by Europeans within Europe is rooted in the violence meted out by Europeans beyond Europe, but why should these thoughts come to me while I am standing in the kitchen staring at the space that was held by the portrait of a jaunty cunt?

Other faces decorate the fridge-freezer. The cat's was carved from a piece of cedar, her tiny green eyes on lookout, her pink mouth a purse of pity. Beside her, Samuel Beckett in black and white. It was shot in 1976. The year of the drought. The year after Franco died. The year my parents took us to Spain in someone else's car. We returned with a barrel of wine hidden beneath the back seat, just scraping through customs thanks to the car-sick child sitting on top of it. I can still see the soldier's eyes reaching through the window. Something ran across his heart and he gently waved us through.

Beckett's gaze is less forgiving. He will not look away. If he cared, he might be imploring me to do what must be done before it is too late. As it is, he aches with regret at my frivolous decision to slap his face between a pussy and a plastic sunflower.

Would he be happier if I created one of those unfinished sentences out of magnetic poetry, arranging the pieces at awkward angles to suggest they are sidling away from his lean top lip? A sort of riff on a riff to show that I am in on the joke, the one you attempted to explain to me, the one I've still not understood, the one about high-culture-meets-low-culture. Anyway, I bought the mini-portrait with serious intent – to remind myself of my admiration for beak man's words, even when I'm standing in the kitchen smashing a slab of pork with a rolling pin.

Sometimes I want to smash his portrait, too, because I'm bored of my Beckett pretensions. I've seen so many fridges with this photo of his face, as if the dead Irishman were some kind of deity, as if the unblinking intelligence oozing from every furrow in his face also oozes from the owner of the fridge.

Oh, I felt such a fraud when Omar bounced into the kitchen and, glancing at the fridge-freezer, released three joyful gusts: Ah! Yes! Beckett! I only wish I'd pulled it from its place right there right then and given it to him to put on his own fridge door.

Years later, here it is, still on show, for anyone to see. Why won't I throw it away? Put it in the bin like the squirrel's skin? Perhaps it is too late. Perhaps it's because his mouth is closed. Because, as he himself said, nothing is sayable. Because everything in this damned world calls for indignation. Even a magnet clinging to a fridge.

Take the miniature bird's-eye view of Liverpool's Metropolitan Cathedral of Christ the King, its construction completed the year you were born. I don't think I reflected fully enough when you told me that your father had entered the competition to design a new cathedral for the city of his birth. He didn't win. Frederick Gibberd did. *Sir* Frederick Gibberd. Born in Coventry, his father a tailor. Your father's father, a riveter, who worked for Cammell Laird at the shipyard in Birkenhead.

I still remember the day we found out that John Laird Sons and Company built a raiding ship for the Confederate States Navy. And that, in 1863, the *Alabama* docked in Cape Town, the town you and I love to loathe. There, she became the subject of an Afrikaans folk song, Daar kom die Alibama, which professors Henry Louis Gates and Emmanuel Kwaku Akyeampong have described as the soundtrack for a wistful conflation of American and Cape histories connected by slave ownership.

In 1864, the *Alabama* was sunk outside Cherbourg, a town I visited to celebrate the achievements of a gynaecologist called Lom. His best friend and lover was a man named Fig. Fig was a classical pianist. He lost a finger during World War II. Ripped off by shrapnel.

The word GAZA follows the curve of the handpainted tile that arrived in London inside a paper bag. It was brought by a man who was born in Brigg. A man who goes to the Occupied Palestinian Territories to help the medics improve their emergency procedures for trauma injuries. It is decorated with a palm tree and a stoic figure riding a camel across the sand.

As if it knows its own history, this ceramic with a magnet glued to its back is chipped in two places. It has a long crack running down the left side and another that meets it across the top. Like so many of our things that end up on the kitchen floor, you glued it back together. But the broken white spaces still insist upon loss.

The first time I held it, I felt quite overwhelmed. I thought about the hands that had made it, and the hands those hands have held, and the lives lived by the owners of all those hands. I thought about the bread that has been torn in those hands, the taps that have been turned and the water that has washed. I thought about the hair that has been untangled between the fingers on those hands, and the wire fences to which they have clung. I thought about the rocks that have been thrown, and the flags that have been waved, the fists of protest that have been formed, and the fires that have been lit. I thought about the scarves that have been tied, and the shirts that have been torn, and all the tears that have been wiped away. I thought about the pages that have been turned, the spoons that have been stirred, the instruments that have been plucked, and the laces that have been pulled. I thought I saw the nostrils that have been poked, the lips that have been touched, and all the Kirby grips that have slid through locks of hair and around folds of cotton and silk. I wondered what was being made with all the threads that have been pushed through all the fixed needles of steel. I saw the screws that have been turned, and the walls into which they have been pushed. I saw the clothes that have been folded and the rings that are still worn. Today, I think about all the eyes that have looked in the direction those fingers have pointed. What would I give to see what they have seen?

Without this broken tile, I might not have appreciated Don Paterson's poem printed in pencil inside your drawer.

> The shudder in my son's left hand
> he cures with one touch from his right,
> two fingertips laid feather-light
> to still his pen. He understands
> the whole man must be his own brother
> for no man is himself alone;
> though some of us have never known
> the one hand's kindness to the other.

Now, I'm watching footage of a hand that shudders beside a border fence in Gaza. I am trying to follow the rubber-coated steel bullets as they fly through the air. I can hear the explosions. I can see the flags and the flames, and I am regretting that I told you a lie.

I'm thinking about the Israeli soldiers, too. About their lovers and their brothers and their mothers and mothers' mothers. All the journeys they have made in their struggle, I suppose they'd say, to feel safe. I often wonder how I have made sense of all the photos I have seen that have filled me with fragments in my life's half-century. Fuzzy thinking about lines of people queuing behind razor-wire, about olive trees being hacked to pieces, and houses built on hills with bedrooms that are watchtowers – and the skateboard park and the beach and the zoo with the mummified animals. The starving lion that gets rescued.

And there is dust from Gaza in our home. It is in the kitchen, it is on the fridge. I have touched this dust! Have I swallowed it, too? Have I swept it up? Is there dust from Gaza on the broom beside the ironing board in the cupboard under the stairs? The broom that brushes over all the trainers that are piled up and muddled up and waiting to go out and run. Have I taken dust from Gaza into Epping Forest and shed it beneath the oak that began to grow while Henry VIII still trod this earth?

I didn't believe you when you told me about the dust that was discovered in the gutters of the roofs of buildings in Berlin and Oslo and Paris. Dust that backs up to the birth of the solar system. Dust that is over four and a half billion years old. Dust that entered the atmosphere at a speed of twelve kilometres per second. The fastest moving dust ever found on earth.

Until you came home with that armful of cornflowers, I'd never heard of the Era of Silence or the Singing Revolution. I didn't know that Estonia was the first country to conduct elections over the internet. I couldn't have named its capital, or located it on a map.

Then you gave me thirty-seven upright green stalks topped with delicacies of copper sulphate blue. You told me what the florist had said: I don't like cornflowers because I don't like the way they die. So I watched them over several weeks transform into locks of long wet hair hanging from the heads of the drowned.

I wondered about the florist. I wondered what he saw.

Over a year has passed and the cornflowers still stand in their vase on the sill. Their bitterness dusts the air when my knuckles knock this tangled mess because I'm reaching for the washing-up liquid or trying to bat the fat black flies bouncing bull-headed off the windowpane.

Some of the petals have held their colour, some have turned to Prussian blue. Some of the buds never opened. They hang at the end of grey-gold threads, dry as drought, entirely dead. Dozens of petals lie scattered around the heavy glass jug. Bleached to ash in the sun on the sill, these fragile florets resemble the frail hands that slid in summer into those white crocheted gloves, so popular between the two world wars.

My pair belonged to an old, old aunt. She smoked twenty a day until, aged ninety-three, she passed away. She never used a cigarette holder and was remembered for her yellow fingertips and her tendency to suck on the threads of tobacco that caught between her top front teeth.

When she died, I longed to slip my hands inside those gloves and smoke. But my bones were already too big to be a lady like that. I couldn't pull the gloves more than half way up my hand, so I placed them inside the wicker basket that had once contained a chocolate egg the size of a child's skull and is now home to three of my dog's milk teeth, a stoat's tail, a pair of Brazilian gaúcho spurs with spikes that spin at the heel, and that copy of the Bible I stole from that motel in the Free State, the one that was run by that husband and wife.

She refused to speak English because of what the British had done during the Anglo-Boer war. He defended her while showing us around the farm. When we reached the garden pond, which was surrounded by ornamental wild animals and toadstools and even a gnome with a fishing rod, all spaced at uncannily regular distances, he turned on us.

I always like to ask our British guests if they have heard of Sir Henry Campbell-Bannerman, he said. When we shook our heads, he explained that he had been the leader of the Liberal Party at the turn of the last century. He segued into a speech.

> When is a war not a war? When it is conducted with the methods of barbarism being deployed against the Boers in South Africa. That's what he said! A British man, in 1901! My wife's ancestors, my ancestors, torn off our land, here, in the Orange Free State. Your ancestors locked us up in their fokken concentration camps!

He stopped. He smiled. His voice dropped. Your concentration camps, he said, glaring into us. Then he pointed to a wooden outhouse with a little terrace and he handed you the key. We serve dinner at eight, he said.

I found the Bible inside the top drawer of the bedside table. Do you remember me lying on the bed with my legs in the air, reading the inscription out loud? It was from 1978. PW Botha, then minister of defence. It was addressed to members of the South African Defence Force.

> This Bible is an important part of your calling to duty. When you are overwhelmed with doubt, pain, or when you find yourself wavering, you must turn to this wonderful book for answers . . . You are now called to play your part in defending our country. It is my prayer that this Bible will be your comfort so that you can fulfil your duty and South Africa and her people will forever be proud of you. Of all the weapons you carry, this is the greatest because it is the Weapon of God.

You were still standing by the door to the terrace, looking out over the domesticated pond to the mountains in the distance.

So are they the Drakensberg? you asked.

The views were so vast, I'd lost all perspective. Before we'd turned off the highway that afternoon, we'd watched three thunderstorms happening all at the same time.

Looking back, I wonder why we didn't spend more time exploring that part of the Free State. We were just kilometres from the site of Kamp Kerkhof, where thousands died from overcrowding, desperately unhygienic conditions and too little food. They weren't all Boers, as our host had implied. Close to 25,000 were Afrikaner farmers, yes, but as many as 20,000 African tenants and labourers also died.

Horatio Herbert Kitchener, who became overall commander of British forces in 1900, was warned about the conditions in the camps. He knew about the Hague Convention of 1899, but chose to ignore the laws of war that prohibited collective punishment and attacks on undefended towns or habitations. In fact, he intended precisely to starve out the local population by setting fire to farm buildings and crops and farm animals, and imprisoning the displaced.

I think I took that Bible to spite that couple. I wanted physical proof that the desire for apartheid was alive and kicking into the cracks of the rainbow nation. Perhaps I also wanted proof of my own facility for hate. And, no, I still haven't worked out an answer to that question you asked. I'm still trying to find my way out of the enclosure of race.

A past that once seemed so distant moves closer the older you get. I was born in 1968, the year the cornflower became the national flower of Estonia. Until 1988, Estonians who wished to celebrate this flower were obliged to paint it red to circumvent the Soviet prohibition of its depiction. This delicate flower, a flower that requires quite particular conditions to thrive, that requires physical support if it is to remain upright for more than a few days, intimidated the rulers of an empire.

Today, the cornflower is the flower of Dulwich College, the south London boys' school that includes among its alumni Nigel Farage. It is also the flower of Austria's far-right Freedom Party. In the 1930s, it was a secret symbol that allowed Austrian Nazis to identify one another. It was also the favourite flower of Queen Victoria's grandson, Kaiser Wilhelm II. He was emperor of Germany when concentration camps were established in Southwest Africa to imprison the Herero and Nama.

The conditions in these camps were even worse than Kitchener's. The death rate was forty-five percent – almost double that in South Africa a few years earlier. By the time the war ended in 1908, which was sixty years before I was born and which will, before long, form a symmetrical point in time with the years I have been alive, the Nama population had halved and only a fifth of the Herero were still alive.

For the past two summers, residents in some of our

neighbouring streets have grown cornflowers in the raised beds they've built around the bases of the silver birches that sway at intervals over the pavements in front of their homes. You think it looks nice. You said it's good that people care. But I call it the boast of bourgeois desire. I mean, digging in bulbs or planting a cutting from a rosemary bush at the base of a tree otherwise surrounded by tarmac is one thing, but raised beds are about borders. They are about ownership, about keeping the passing pedestrian out. They invite envy. They invite you to compete. They invite you to admire this mini-garden, to desire this politely tended street.

As far as the dog is concerned, a raised bed is the ideal spot for a pee. He has always preferred to urinate on soil rather than tarmac or concrete because there is no splash back. Pissing on soil with a fixed wooden border is even better because the trickle is contained and a puddle does not form so his pads and his toes stay dry.

When it comes to defecating, the dog has always shown a preference for shitting either onto or off a ledge. He particularly likes kerbs. He likes their smooth surface. In summer, he likes the stone of the kerb because it is cooler than the hot black tarmac or the concrete slabs of the main path. He likes to stand on the edge and defecate into the drain in the gutter. I've watched him back up, crouch down and open his bowels so accurately over a drain cover that the faeces fall freely between the cast iron bars without even brushing their sides.

I have begun to dissect my dead cornflowers. I have begun to pull them apart. A dessicated calyx lies in my palm. This cryptic crown, which was once green and elegant and held the blue flower so firmly from beneath, is now a circle of tiny spears, each dipped in poison. The tip of every sepal has curled and turned black, as if someone had come at night and delicately stitched dark thread around the edge of each thorny, yellowing leaf. When I break the calyx in two, I see that I am holding a small pair of gloves made from the skin of a dead woman's hands.

My mind flickers with the old Russian woman who died in her flat in St Petersburg when her sixty-eight-year-old lodger, also a woman, poisoned her favourite salad, an Olivier, with phenazepam. Her body was chopped into pieces. Her head was boiled in a pan.

I'm looking at the gloves you bought me when I helped that old lady from Albania move home. The one who married the man who walks the streets in a hi-vis vest, who likes to talk about his long-haired German Shepherd. The first time we met, he grabbed the top of my arm and pushed his nails into my skin. He said he'd been forced to give the dog away after neighbours complained to the police about its bark. His Galway accent felt defeated when he whispered into my sternum, You won't say I didn't warn you.

His words came back to me when I was in their back garden, pulling on the gloves, which were blue and rubber and far too tight. I was stepping between a tidy pair of rose bushes, I was trying to avoid the sacks of manure. When I noticed the laceration across my left palm, I whispered to the plants, Slashed by that old woman with a knife! It was only then that I gave the word glove my full attention. It was only then that I noticed it encompasses love.

I hold no affection for the washing machine. I hate the bucket that came with the mop. I recoil from the dustpan and the brush, the ironing board, and the pair of extra-strong rubber gloves you like to tuck into that dark space we didn't know existed until you lost the cat. You were so panicked, you rang me in Spain. You held the tremor down your throat when you told me, She's vanished.

Later that evening, while perched on the loo, you heard two tiny cries. You dropped to your knees and followed the sound, and you found her, curled into the hole behind the great white bowl. With trousers around your ankles, you pulled her out and you pushed the gloves in, blocking the entrance should she attempt to make her return.

Those gloves. Why do I assume they are for women's hands? Is this why I bristle at the fluffy yellow dusters, too, and the can of Mr Sheen? I have seen many things in my life. I have seen a Harris hawk swoop on a magpie on a footpath on an east London industrial estate, and drag it through the fence into a furniture factory. I have seen a kingfisher follow the River Lea south to the Olympic site and, a few miles north, a colourful cock pheasant land clumsily on the edge of the Tottenham marsh. I have seen a sparrowhawk plummet from a plane tree into a suburban privet and emerge with a bird in its claws. I have seen my dog hunt a hare at full pelt only to run straight over it when it flattened itself into the soil, vanished and still on the earth. I have seen lions and rhinos, and I have touched the skin of a moving elephant. I have seen the crawling crocodiles of Yamoussoukro, and I have read, in my own inbox, the rage of the readers of the *Daily Mail*. I have driven through the smoke of a forest fire, and I have shouted at three white police officers who were sitting on the body of my young black neighbour, face down flat out in our street. I have looked through the window of another neighbour's house and seen a middle-aged man kneeling naked on his kitchen floor, immersed in the sonic space of Bora Yoon. But I have never seen a man shaking Mr Sheen, or taking a yellow cloth to a bookshelf or a banister or a mantel above a fire.

Close to the smoke alarm, where the narrow red pipes vanish into plaster, there is a part of the downstairs ceiling where the globules of fat that turn women into insomniacs seem to emerge from the scars of the old dining-room wall. A wall we never touched. A wall that was built under Queen Victoria and knocked down under

Thatcher. And when I lie on the sofa, trying to translate the heaving in my heart, I cannot resist imagining the accumulation of their blotched buttocks and pale hips. Like pancake batter that's been thrown at the wall, it thickens and bubbles, goes goose-grey with time. Gazing upwards, staring in, I think I can see the line of Thatcher's knicker hem. I can trace the track where the elastic meets her flesh. The softness, the squidge. The chilblains that crack the skin, which peels and curls and crumbles in her tights. Yes, here I am, lying long on red, following the folds of Thatcher's flesh. Do I dare touch her apricot nipple? Run a finger to her pit?

Might this moment motivate me to harm? Like your diabolical aunt. She took in stray cats. Dozens of them, year after year, purring and preening, prowling around her lawn. She fed them steamed fish and chopped-up chicken she'd boiled the same day. She gave them milk and thick cream.

When it came to winter, when it was cold and ice crisp, she'd place the dishes inside the pantry and wedge the door with a short block of wood. A soft towel inside the washing-machine encouraged the cats to take shelter and curl.

Nesting, she called it, just like birds.

Stupid birds, I said, the first time you told me the story. No one washes a folded towel.

Every year, before winter was through, she would wake one morning, unusually ripe, and patter downstairs to catch the cats sleeping in their nest. She would close the machine door. She would set the dial to a hot cotton wash and watch the water rise and rise, and as it began to froth white with soap, she held her fingernails to the convex window and scratched at the screaming pets trapped on the other side.

Cat Murder Day, she called it. An annual event.

I never wanted this washing machine. I like laundrettes too much. I like the smell that wafts out of large tumble-dryers, their flat transparent doors re-assuring at rib height. I like sitting on the bench watching the clothes rise and twist and fall - remembering the leaves that never settle, that are blown into the air over and over again by an off-screen wind machine, positioned presumably just behind the camera, in that very long Hungarian film we saw.

I like looking for my knickers and trying to spot your socks, and wishing that I, too, could be lifted and turned inside the feathered, warm air. Wishing that I, too, could be fluffed up.

I like putting my coins into the slot. That sense of accomplishment when you hear them drop. That split of silence just before the drum starts revolving again, and the vision of the vending machine outside the changing rooms at the public swimming pool – of wrapped-up chocolate falling behind glass.

I like the conversations that unfold with other people. Their stories about their dogs. One in particular, the man with gold teeth. He'd park up early in a silver soft-top. Upright beside him, a substantial Rottweiler, all bushy black tail. He'd dump his washing into one of the machines, slap in the cash, then whistle like a Welshman calling a Collie down the hill. This tank of a dog would leap from the car and charge into the laundrette, sliding to a horizontal at his master's spotless Nike feet.

The first time I saw this I stood up to clap and he turned and he asked me if I'd ever taught a dog to bark. I hesitated. Watch! he said. He took three long steps back from the dog and raised his right hand. Four fingers and a thumb spread wide. The dog responded with such a loud bark, the vibrations bounced off the machines and sharpened a spike of fear. The man twisted round to look at me. Eye to eye. He grinned and turned back to his dog.

This time, he dropped the thumb, showing the animal just the four fingers. Again, the animal replied with a bark, this one not quite as loud as the first. When he showed the dog three fingers, the bark was softer still. Two fingers, even softer – and a little higher in pitch. Finally, he showed the dog one solitary finger. This time, he woofed so sweetly he barely parted his lips. Very useful that, said Goldie, weaving his fingers through his keys.

A few months later, a petrol bomb was lobbed into the flat above the laundrette. The whole building burned to the ground. I was living with a lodger. He liked to smoke in bed. He told me to buy a washing machine. Living without one is not normal, he said.

So I bought a Hotpoint Spin Washer Dryer on a two-year hire purchase deal. It was a beautiful object. A slippery, cumbersome cube. I like to think that I appreciated the engineering, the accumulation of skill. But cleaning clothes became a silent and solitary, labour-saving experience. Every wash felt sad.

The thing is, I like a bit of labour. I feel complete when I get down on my hands and knees on the kitchen floor. I take real pleasure retrieving the large sponge from the cupboard beneath the sink. It's genuine excitement when I reach behind the curled pipe to pull out the square bucket, its original sunshine yellow disguised beneath layers of Hammerite washed from the brush you used to paint seven televisions gold.

The sight of you standing before that sculpture of abandoned pallets – all that glue and expanding foam, your gold trousers, the glittered top, the silver ring in your left lobe – it drips into me as I locate the floor-cleaning soap in its glossy green bottle that feels on my fingers like the gelatin glaze from a fruit tart on my tongue.

The soap itself is a transparent treacle of such viscosity that even when the bottle is inverted, it refuses to fall in one heavy dollop. It must be coaxed and encouraged. Finally, forced. Still, it slides as slowly as the Spanish slugs that appear every year on the kitchen floor. Fat fingers of orange secreting lines of slime while following one another in their search for sex somewhere on these tiles.

These tiles, laid in 1885. Down here, on all my fours, the heels of my hands pushing into the nicks of history. If we had been alive then, you would have been the exhausted man on your knees scrubbing the wide back of your wife, sitting in the tin tub beside the back door. Her head resting on her knees, her eyes fixed on the cast-iron range set into the fireplace. It is late March. Still cold. She's thinking about coal. She's not thinking about the partition of Africa. About the Conference of Berlin. Of lines being drawn like the lines between these tiles.

These quarry tiles, made of red rock strata over four hundred million years old. These tiles that I like to clean. Upon which I like to watch my large hands working and wet. To see the sponge squeezed at its waist. My arm moving forward and back and round and up and down and over to the side, creating planets and rainbows and shapes of shells. These tiles that are territories, each within its border, each one carved square and discrete.

My crimson knuckles working freely on this kitchen floor that was laid one hundred and thirty-five years ago, the year that King Leopold II declared by royal decree the État Indépendant du Congo. Even more cruelly in English, the Congo Free State. Bent over these wet red tiles, I'm trying to understand the meaning of these words. I'm wondering whether there will ever come a day when I cannot remember the image of those two boys. They are looking straight into the lens, their hands hacked off.

I must have held my breath the first time, but I did not look away. My gaze tunnelled into the abyss.

Now, I reach for my magnifying glass. A single lens held in a tortoiseshell frame that slips in and out of a stiff leather sheath. Strange to be holding this piece of glass over this monochrome, each made at the turn of the last century.

I look closer and closer, and even closer still. My nose a few inches from theirs. The younger boy – his eyelids heavy with horror, his face fading, his body weak – stands like a ghost beside the older boy, who is sitting stunned on a chair, his eyes wide and wet.

Many times I have wondered what became of this pair.

And why, oh why, does my mind leap to the sight of a naked man on all fours on his bedroom floor?

Must I admit to this?

Close behind him, between his parted legs, a second man is kneeling naked, making shapes with his hand. He's throwing the shadow of a swan at the wall. Its long neck jerks backwards and forwards, striding towards the other man's arse. It arrives and inspects and pushes its beak between his cheeks. Eyes closed, it snuffles forward, through the anus, into the rectum.

Deep inside. Gasps.

The first time you took me back to your home city, we stood at the gates of Cammell Laird. We gazed at the warehouse and the concrete, and the cracks where the buddleia grew. I looked for ships, and saw a vast red skip piled high with pieces of discarded computers and speakers and mobile phones. Green printed circuit boards were glinting in the sun. Tiny bits of metal shining like the view from the sky of the city at night. Standing there, our faces pressed between metal bars, fingers curled round wire, I tried to harness the history of this place.

Bespoke ships built in Birkenhead. Ships that dominated the trans-Atlantic trade in humans enslaved. Ships that carried all the cargo in and out of the Congo.

Weapons went in.

Hands, arms, strips of lips and ears and slices of skin were hacked off.

Ivory and rubber came out.

The voices that tumbled into my ears during that first trip north formed a language unknown. We were under the ground when I looked to you and you repeated their words for their words in an accent you knew I knew. I was a foreigner. I felt entirely content. You showed me streets with every other home hammered down, every orifice nailed shut. Zones so rejected, there were houses on sale for a pound. I looked at these lives and saw myself exposed.

You led me over the Mersey to show me the shipyard, to show me the labour of your grandad's life. We navigated wide roads and a retail park with a McDonald's drive-thru. We entered on foot. We bought servings of fries and a chocolate shake that contained so much sugar it gave us the shakes. I got dizzy and you made me sit on the verge beside the tarmac. Together, we watched cars. We talked about saliva and slavery and serotonin, and you reminded me of the time I crashed my bike near a fish-and-chip shop because I'd sucked too many lemon sherbets. You said you'd take me to Mother Noblett's Toffee Shop. Makers of the original Everton Mint. Your father's mother had been the manageress. She'd travelled the country selling mints. She was half-Croatian. She'd married your father's father because he had lovely skin. Like a baby's, you said she'd said.

I lay on the grass and I listened to your voice, to your gentle memories of sculling the West Float, of pulling oars beneath Royal Navy combat store ships, of rowing through rolling fog, of the morning you saw the angel under the water and the big black dog beside the red brick wall.

You reminisced about rowing at Runcorn and races against a boy who was six foot six and had dark hair and didn't say much. Nor did you, but you were blonde and five foot ten, and he had the better boat. A Janousek, you said, and you muttered about carbon fibre and coloured chevrons and the fact the boats were always white. Janousek was Czech, you said. He revolutionised the sport. But no one bothered to learn his name. Instead, they called him Bob.

In 1983, you won what you like to call the Nat Champs. When I asked you what you'd won, you reminded me of the silver tankard standing on the shelf beneath your three guitars, including the bass your cousin built in 1974 when she was into glam rock.

Inside the tankard are three medals. One hangs from a burgundy ribbon and is covered in mould. I love looking at it, at your name engraved in capital letters. Your fungal bling.

Folded up beneath the medals, a piece of paper burned brown in the sun. On one side, three words, like Gods, in blue, Neusilin Neuphane Neulente. On the other, your handwriting in gold:

> To Yossarian, the idea of pennants as prizes was absurd. No money went with them, no class privileges. Like Olympic medals and tennis trophies, all they signified was that the owner had done something of no benefit to anyone more capably than everyone else.

As Coventry is twinned with Volgograd, so your silver tankard is twinned with a moth trap. Its adhesive surface ripples and glistens, a little like Monet's lake with the water-lilies, a thought that occurred to me when I saw someone talking about the artist on the *Antiques Roadshow*. But the gloss of the glue on the moth trap has been ploughed with the straight strokes of a machine, not the hand of a man working for years to capture the reflection on water of the sun and the clouds.

Held within a piece of plastic not quite the whitest of whites, this kit for killing is a monument to shadow and light. The longer I look at it, the more convinced I am it was created by Louis I. Kahn. A by-product of the Jatiya Sangsad Bhaban, the huge parliament complex he designed for Bangladesh. Not that I know much about the great architect, beyond a few facts.

I know that he was born Leiser-Itze Schmuilowksy in Estonia in 1901. I know that, as a toddler, he burned his face after picking up hot coals from the fire, having been attracted by their light. And I know that, in 1906, his family emigrated to the States, to Philadelphia's Jewish ghetto, where they lived in and out of poverty. I also know that I admire his devotion to geometric shapes. I love the way his lines recede from circles, the way he frames circles inside squares. And I know that I can ask this piece of plastic, What do you do, plastic? And plastic replies, I like an arch.

I keep having these moments when I think I can see Kahn's scarred face. He's standing at a desk, a thick pencil in hand. His eyes are softening and he's drawing an opening of some sort. It's inspired by the grapefruits he released into a bowl. When the circle is complete, he surrounds it with six arches, each modelled on the wider end of the pale blue egg that was laid by the lone Cream Legbar pecking about next door. Inside this sculpted hangar, beneath the symmetry of simple shapes, shadows come and go beside small blocks of light. Even the most reluctant eye could not resist to gaze upon its surface – almost unbearably smooth, like the poured resin suffocating the kitchen floors of those who stroll on London's fields.

The first time I encountered this type of moth trap, I was browsing in a large shop beneath the tarmac of Oxford Street. I passed a personalised dog bowl made from oak and stainless steel and priced at a hundred and fifty-five pounds. The emphasis here, in this flattened space, was upon a sterile aesthetics of home, upon the appearance of absolute hygiene, upon a certain discretion of death.

Far better to turn to Kahn, who believed that a room has religion, that a room is a world within a world. He believed that we are all made of spent light. We all have something to express, from microbe to moth to machine and man. He believed that before a building is built, there exists a tremendous will and that, at this stage of nothingness, the building is at its best. Once it is built, it is locked in servitude. It wants to tell you how it was built, but can find no one to listen.

A building is only good, thought Kahn, if its ruins will be any good. He was discouraged by those who thought about buildings in terms of functionality. A building is a spirit, he said. It is made out of man.

A moth trap is a spirit too, I say, and it is made of man.

A slice of the sun filters through the space of the trap, which lures in life and sticks it still. These tiny moths, these delicate creatures, whose wings are made of silver silk, their bodies threaded with gold. The moth trap holds tight in glue these beautiful, shimmering things. Stuck down, they turn brown. They will never fly nor flutter again, these creatures with their extravagant, feminine name.

Should Tineola bisselliella not die upon gold leaf?

I only noticed the precious metal moths after I'd been polishing the tankard and got side-tracked wondering whether I still had a mind of my own. I was standing at a table that was covered with a cloth of boiled wool. The room was darkening when I lifted the pot of silver polish wadding in one hand and, with the other, began to twist its smooth circular lid. I closed my eyes for the sensation of metal sliding into metal, for the satisfaction of the suction, of molecules colliding between my hands. I pulled at the folds of the crab-pink wadding, which stuck to my fingers like wet candy floss. I rubbed it into the curves of the silver until it oozed with liquid like blood and dirty oil. The tankard in my hands, now slippy, still hard, became the arm of a man, head bowed on flat wood. The back of the cleaver comes down on the back of the cleaver, its blade held in place by a man with a long beard.

I'm looking at my own hands now, at these gloves, turquoise blue. I think of the Congo, I think of Mosul, Iraq.

My thoughts shift shamefully back to the man's arm twisting inside the other man's arse, to a woman pushing her whole hand up inside herself. Further back still to the woman we watched on stage. Do you remember her laughing? And the baby dying, and the soldier, who was slumped on the floor, his brains splattered on the wall. Another man was on his knees, shuffling back and forth. He could not see because his eyes had been sucked out by the soldier, who'd raped him with his gun and with the stump that was all that remained of his thigh. Then the woman buried the baby and she went to look for food. While she was gone, the man with no eyes dug up the child and tore into its flesh with his teeth. When the woman returned she was singing.

But what disturbed me most that night was the audience. They'd wanted a happy ending. They'd wanted the play to give them hope. They didn't want to know that it was written by a woman who hanged herself with the lace of a shoe.

I could stab myself with my hairpin. It is long and beautifully sharp. A fist that rises from an arrow of sandalwood. I bought it because its caramel colour triggered the taste of toffee on my tongue. In my fingers it felt slender and smooth. I bought it because I wanted to wear a symbol of struggle in my hair. It was lying on a table on a piece of cotton cloth. The contained chords of Nelson Mandela's voice flickered somewhere in my head. The lips of Malcolm X. In black and white. On film.

Now, I see the raised arm of Agostinho Neto, the first president of independent Angola. Now, the gaps between his front teeth. Those strange spaces of imperfection seem to make him more vulnerable than I've previously allowed. Are the struggles led by African men, led by African American men, my struggles too?

When I look at my hairpin, I never think of a white man's fist. But when I force myself to consider such a fist, it is always a fascist's fist. When I twist my hair and poke the pin up and round and over, as it slides down the back of my scalp, it becomes a weapon in waiting. I wonder what force would be required to push it clean into the chest of a man, to the side of his sternum between two ribs? To get a better grip, I could wear my rubber gloves. Perhaps it would be simpler to force it into the soft side of his wrist? Or through the wet flesh of his warm cheek, where the blood will find his throat?

When I slide the hairpin back and forth between the tip of my left finger and the flat surface of my thumb, I become a cellist running a bow along a long and bendy saw. When I push the sharpened point underneath my fingernail, into the zone called the hyponychium, I feel a swell of satisfaction as I ease out the dirt that has accumulated with the companionship of a dog.

Beneath the bed, another weapon, the length of my lower leg. This one, more obvious, is made from galvanised steel. I like the word galvanised. It brings on Mr Spock and the pointy bump at the top of my ear. I miss the belief that I am really part Vulcan. I miss the fear I felt when I wanted to get a gun. Fear does not explain the piece of scaffold piping beneath the bed. I was excited by the possibility of seeing you hold it like a baseball bat and swing it at an intruder's head. I'm still looking forward to the sound that might make.

If I knock it with my knuckles while it's resting on my

lap, unreliable memories of Saharan sheep merge with a video of Alpine ibex leaping up the side of a sheer stone dam to lick wet mineral salts. But the prettiest notes my body makes in collaboration with this scaffold pipe are when I play it like a piano with my weak, winter nails. Like the rain falling on the little metal bin that we still fill with ashes from the fire. The fire with its poisoning particulates. The wet wood in the shed.

If I take this pole in both my hands and set my gaze upon the steel, I see ghostly forms and silvery hoods moving through the swarm. I long for Ablade Glover, for his Accra gallery beside the sea. His large canvases crammed with bodies, buying, selling, shuffling and sweating in a wide West African market that might melt in the expanding heat.

But the bodies that haunt my scaffold pole are trampling the earth with fear. There is murmuring and whispering. There are plenty who weep. A man with heavy Mediterranean hands has his arm around the shoulders of his son, who is slender and unsure, who knows his father is afraid. Two girls are walking with their elbows linked. Their heads are leaning in, pressed against one another, wishing they could become one.

Rolling the pole over my desk, the crowd never ends. The mood is increasingly solemn. Even when I turn away, then quickly twist to look back, there's always this woman, her hair as thick as a honey badger's pelt. She's standing stock-still, neck stretched high, scanning the buildings for a sniper who'll fire.

I roll the pole back and forth, enjoying the reliable quality of metal on my skin. I recognise that I am both sniper and snipe. I rest the muzzle of my rifle on the rotting wooden sill of the old lead windows above the working men's club that was converted into a pair of share-to-buy flats. I know that when I shoot her it won't be that deflated experience of shooting flattened aluminium ducks at the fair before an audience of adolescent males all trying to ignore their spikes of jealousy every time I hit another and another and another fake duck dead.

The shock of outshining boys may be wedged into my flesh like shrapnel, but who doesn't want to hold a real gun? Who has no desire to fire it – to feel, in the tip of a single finger, the satisfaction of squeezing a well-designed trigger? If there is any melancholy here, it comes from the knowledge that the common snipe is a finely camouflaged wading bird with a beak longer than its legs, and a tail with feathers that fan in flight to send unnerving electronic sounds to an enigmatic planet.

When we first met, there was something about you that resembled, to my mind, Derek Jarman. You were walking with a stick and you wore a cotton hat. Those first few hours, you smiled a lot. We both rolled cigarettes and sat cross-legged and ate pieces of chocolate that you'd cooked with cannabis leaves. In your bedsit, we climbed a ladder to the top of a scaffold of steel. Raised to the ceiling, this was your bed. Below, a dark cave housed your desk and a chair, an orange Apple Mac and an old-fashioned camera and a basket full of clothes. I recall a rotary dial telephone in a shade of clotted cream.

For over an hour, I watched you on a call to your mother. She discussed the dog's obesity and her wish to alter her will. You barely said a word. Your head sunk lower and lower, and I looked at the shapes in the sheets of purple silk and the strips of black nylon that were pinned to the wall. There was blue velvet too, and I wondered where you'd bought it and why you liked to cocoon yourself down there in the dark.

Up the ladder, you brought me black coffee and grapefruit concentrate. We ate toast above that scaffolding. We made love and watched the albino Staffie beneath the apple tree in the vast, overgrown garden out the back.

The other day, I was reading old news from Tehran. Five men were publicly hanged from simple structures of scaffold poles. They belonged to a group called the Black Vultures. They raped and robbed women. Two of the men were hanged at a bus terminal in the west of the city. The other three were hanged in Lavizan, a neighbourhood in the north-east. Some of their supporters set off home-made hand grenades. There were families watching the hangings from their rooftops. Youngsters nibbled crisps. The mother of one of the men fainted twice. The bodies were left hanging for over half an hour.

If there were public executions here, I know now, without a flicker of doubt, that I would want to attend. I would want to witness murder by the state. I would want to experience my body's response. I would not want to turn my back or cover my eyes and my ears. I would want to know, deep inside myself, how a public execution would affect my body and mind. Would it do me any good? Would you come too?

When we visited that house on the hill, I stood in a room filled with etchings by Marcelle Hanselaar and Paula Rego. In one, a dog was lying on its back, a naked woman on her knees. She was rubbing her vulva against the dog's balls. A man wore a colander as a helmet on his head. A thick scarf had been wound round his neck. In the distance, a line of men in heavy coats and trilbies was marching into a low brick building. Vantablack smoke seeped through the cracks in the roof. The dog began to howl. A monkey stroked the woman's back. Everyone had thick tongues. In one corner, an older woman with leaking eye make-up was binding another woman in ribbons of red silk.

Through the window, I saw a tall figure leave the house. Her hair was white with a blade of orange beside each ear. When I tracked her down some weeks later, I discovered that she, too, had her bed raised high on scaffold poles. Unlike you, she didn't take new lovers up the ladder. I've had a couple roll out, she said, so I break them in on the floor.

I've been practising rolling across our mattress, reaching underneath the bed and grabbing the sawn-off scaffold. The hardest part is crawling out from beneath the duvet without making much noise and, as quickly as possible, getting into a standing position from which to swing the thing emphatically at his head. He's always the same man: hamster jacket, inconsequential blue jeans, dense patches of ginger stubble. Thin.

In my head, I've tried to hit him so many times, I've worked out exactly where I need to place my feet in order to strike him on the forehead whilst avoiding smashing the flame-shaped lightbulbs that rise from the antique brass structure that was fixed to the ceiling by Dudley.

Dudley and his charcoal monobrow. The dense silver hair on his head, and the slowness that hypnotised us as he leafed through the electrics catalogue for bathroom extractor fans. Page by page by page by page. In another life, Dudley might have been a guru. It was Dudley who left the hole I've looked at all these years. All these years, on my back, in our bed, gazing up at Dudley's hole. I've still not stood on a chair and put my finger inside to feel for the note that Dudley wrote.

I have put my fingers inside the long hole of the scaffold pole. This grey tunnel of metal nudges my thoughts to the underpass beneath the circular cinema on the south side of Waterloo Bridge. Unleash Your Power commands a massive glossy billboard just a few feet from half a dozen people, who are trying to sleep inside sodden bags beside piss and puddles and stoical dogs and pieces of cardboard that plead for understanding: I'm not alcohlic please HELP.

What if we all had to declare ourselves in five words on the side of a damp box? If we had to spend days holding messages in front of our sex?

When I hold the scaffold pipe, when I slide my fingers into the dark, it becomes part of me. Even if I rejected it, if I chucked it in a skip, we would forever remain conjoined.

When I examine the bits of horn torn from my toes, I wonder if I, too, am but a thing.


Salvador Dalí was dying of heart failure the day I turned twenty-one. He was in Catalonia. He was eighty-four and he was listening to Wagner, to *Tristan and Isolde*. I did not know then that when he gazed into Hitler's face, the Spanish surrealist saw a moonlit landscape. One nostril is a gentle wooden rowing boat floating close to the riverbank. A single wooden oar, which might be the mast, rises from the centre of the boat, held by an invisible figure that might be a ghost. Someone is standing further up the bank. Tiny, but erect, their shadow cast towards the bottom right-hand corner of the frame. The moon at dusk forms the tip of Hitler's nose. The flat surface of the lake, his nasolabial fold.

While gazing at three pairs of black knickers drying in a row on the red radiator downstairs, I realised I was looking at Hitler's fringe. Because each pair was slightly overlapping the next, together they formed what at first struck me to be a toupée. A block of black hair swept to one side, save a single lock – one thigh hole hanging slightly lower, slightly looser, than all the rest. It brought to my mind the narrow finger of Hitler's forelock trembling above his eye as he stands behind a lectern, rising on his toes and shouting, his left thumb tucked tight against the palm of his hand.

These were my favourite knickers. They made me feel at once athletic and stern. Every now and then, they opened the way to what I can only describe as my inner boy. The relief was real. But for some time now, whenever I pull them over my feet, around my ankles and all the way up my legs to my arse, I cannot escape the thought that they are the hair that grew from Hitler's scalp. Once they are on, nicely snug, all smoothed out, I feel less that my cunt is stretched over Hitler's head, than his skull is trapped between my thighs, his hair caught between my jelly cheeks.

Nevertheless, the joy I felt when I first came across these knickers online has not completely vanished. I still get excited when I locate them among the bras and socks and colourful pairs of pants on the top shelf. It is only when I point my toes, readying to poke them through each hole, that I start to question who I am and what on earth I think I'm doing. It is only then that the führer's face inserts itself into my day.

The radiator on which these knickers were hanging is a double-panel convector radiator. It is large, though not as large as that television that no one ever seems to watch – the one which throws out noise and light all night from the ground floor flat at the bottom of our street. I have been convinced that the man inside is beating someone up, that he turns up the volume to muffle the screams, but the woman over the road – the one who is always leaving oven-proof dishes full of chicken legs and chopped potato in the gutter, the one who takes her oxygen tank for slow walks around the block – well, she says he lives alone.

The radiator's outer panel is formed of thirty-three lean trapezoid forms. The man who eventually agreed to paint the whole thing red was certain it should be replaced with a more fashionable model with oval columns. I regret that I never encouraged him to sit down in front of ours, to study its form with his dark brown eyes. I wish I'd invited him to focus on the vertical lines, to watch them slithering out of reach. If only I'd attempted to articulate my delight at the way the panel traps the light and nudges it, line by line, into dark. The way it will keep moving. The way I have come close to worshipping these uniform shapes and their shuffling shadows when I walk across the room intending to make tea or light a fire or straighten Bernie's painting of the sea or tickle the dog's thigh or stroke the top of your head and the back of your neck or straighten the lamp or shake the rug or puff up the cushions or change the CD or remove a cobweb or scratch my nail into that patch of ceiling that keeps curling damp.

When Terry Waite was kidnapped, he was chained to a radiator for months on end, sometimes for twenty-three hours a day. There are children who still get tied to radiators. And women. Once, I tied a dog to a radiator. Long ago, I remember sitting on a radiator and being told that I'd get piles and wet my pants and that I might make myself infertile.

The first time I saw the photograph *socks on radiator 1998* I fell in love with Wolfgang Tillmans. It was an exhibition at the Tate. We returned home and I spent the evening looking more carefully than ever before at each of our radiators. I discovered a drying-up cloth down the back of the small white one in the kitchen. It must have been there for years because I didn't recognise it when we finally hooked it, you and I together, both holding wooden spoons. I used the one that looks a little like a paddle, the one your mother bought from that woman, who was dressed in green and who said she was homeless, who played that beautiful tune on her flute. It was just before

Christmas. Your mother talked about that woman for the rest of the day.

The drying-up cloth was coated in violet dust. We ran our fingers into it and kissed.

When I look at the red radiator, I can't forget the painter's words. He was so pugnacious. It's the wrong red! he said. When I told him that I liked the wrong red, but didn't like the way I'd heard him talking about Black people and Jews, he shouted at me: Albanians are not racist! We protected the Jews during World War Two!

I wish I'd asked him about King Zog I, and whether it was true that Ian Fleming helped him into exile in the Chiltern Hills? And did he really smoke two hundred cigarettes a day?

Usually, it's the painter's voice that comes first. That bubble in his throat. I'm almost at the top of the stairs, about to set foot on to the landing, to enter the space where he was standing on our ladder, when I hear his xenophobic rant rolling out. It never occurred to me to take seriously anything he said. Not until a year or so later. I was in The Photographers' Gallery. I was trying to still my mind. In the shop in the basement, I came across a book full of portraits of Albanians, mostly Muslims, who took huge risks to protect hundreds of Jews from the occupying German forces. The book takes its title, *Besa*, from the Albanian code of honour. Besa requires that you never betray your neighbours or your guests. It might even require that you risk your child's life in order to save the life of another.

Lime Balla was in her nineties when she met the photographer who created the book. She told him how her family had taken in three brothers in 1943. All of us villagers were Muslims, she said. We were sheltering God's children under our besa. She sits deep in a wide armchair, a blanket on her lap. Resting on her breast is, I think, a copy of the Qu'ran. In her fingers, she holds what might be a small glass of sherry. A white scarf frames her face. It is made of such delicate material that the corners running over her shoulders look like liquid milk. She wears spectacles, but you can tell from her eyes she is as tough as they come. She could swing an axe at a tree and bring it down, no doubt.

I wish I had been there to witness her response when two of the brothers made contact with her again. They were in Israel. It was 1990. Forty-seven years had passed since they left her village and travelled to Kosovo. Forty-seven years since they last spoke.

Standing here, in front of the cooker, peering down on the black grates that straddle the hob, swastikas are what I see. Looking at the dials, turning on the gas, who could fail to consider the camps?

On this stove, I have singed the hair on my head and swallowed the flavour as it moves through the air. I've placed the polished kettle on to the flame and waited for the water to move. There's a need to prepare the mind for pain, to confront the agony of a fingernail being lifted with pliers and torn out, to resist collapse when a hand is held in boiling water, or when the face is pressed into a toaster burning red. When I look through our oven door at the chicken roasting inside, I cannot erase from the prints in my mind Marie Moravec's head. As part of the Czech resistance, she was the woman who provided a safe house for the men who conducted Operation Anthropoid. When the Gestapo arrived at her home in Prague, she swallowed a capsule of cyanide. Her husband and their seventeen-year-old son were captured. The boy was forced to drink brandy to the point of collapse, whereupon a fish tank was brought before him. Floating inside, his mother's head.

On the kitchen windowsill, an old mustard jar holds dregs of pomace brandy and layers of fried-up fat. Sinking somewhere inside this honeyed mix are the bloated bodies of three dead ticks. Each one plucked from the dog with a device so simple you'd not believe the times I've looked at it and caught myself wondering, What would I do without you? When I remove it from its sleeve, a surge of confidence slides up my thumb. I'm always keen to caress its flat blue back. Fixed into the broader end is a wire loop that rises and curls, like a scorpion's tail about to dart its prey.

There is a knack to trapping ticks. I've even pulled one from the dog's eyelid and I am certain that he appreciated my satisfaction, my glee, at the little animal I'd hooked, eight legs and head and all. There is something thrilling about an arachnid hanging in the air, something astonishing about handling a tick. Being together, close enough to touch.

Ticks have been around for millions of years. Ticks have a proboscis that is covered in barbs. Ticks harpoon the animal's skin and fire into its flesh, like ancient ancestors to the ultra-deep oil and gas rigs that drill down thousands of metres into Earth's oligocene.

I have enough black sand to fill an egg cup. It is kept in a glass jar on the narrow white shelf just above my desk. I took it from a beach not far from the Congo river. I was with my minder, Senhõr Gime. He wore impressively pointy shoes and asked me if I knew why the sand was black. Oil! he said. Petroleum sand! he said. I had my doubts, which I now regret. I lacked the will to ask a stronger question because I was enjoying listening to him reminiscing about the old days when the mermaids came ashore.

They dressed in white, he said, but it's rare to see them now. He blamed offshore oil spills and plastic pollution, as well as the curse of fornicating naked couples. A woman and a man should make love in a bed, he said, not rolling around on the ground.

I looked at his shoes, I wanted to laugh, but the terrain held me back.

We stood side by side, gazing out to sea, listening to the water rolling gently on to the beach. As the sun disappeared behind the Atlantic, I followed the line of Senhōr Gime's finger which pointed to an orange flame rising out of the ocean. Flares and gas, he said, flames and platforms. Oil is our only employer. Oil and the army. He pulled a small plastic bag from his pocket and thrust it into my hand. Get yourself some sand, he said, and make sure to remember me.

I carried that sand for many weeks. Several long journeys covering thousands of miles. Eventually, I brought it back home and spooned it into a short, square pot with a fat, firm cork. I placed it on my desk, where it has remained ever since. I look at it as some might look at a photograph of a lover, or a mother, or a child who left home long ago. I look at the sand and I wonder about all it must have witnessed. The middle passage.

How long does sand remain on a beach? Is there such a thing as new sand, or is all sand old sand?

I still think about Senhōr Gime, but can no longer find the detail on his face. I still see his shoes and admire his height. I still wonder about the anxiety in his stoop. Is he alive? Is he well? Does he still think of me as I do him? I remember the shape of his body, the upper half slumped over a desk, sleeping, snoring, almost a purr.

Exhausted in the heat, he took me on a journey along the top of the cliffs. On and on until the sun was setting and we arrived at a pair of green gates in front of which an old man sat crumpled upon a stone. At the sound of the engine, he slowly uncurled. From the front of our battered Land Rover we watched this pile of clothes come to life. I never doubted it: he had always been here. His tongue was so dry, we had to wait for him to produce adequate saliva to loosen it and speak.

He led us to a house, to a padlocked front door. From the top pocket of his shirt, he produced a single key. Inside, Senhōr Gime told me a tale about the man who built the place. Out walking on the beach one day, he came across a beautiful young woman sleeping beside the sea. He picked her up and carried her across the sand, up the rocks, to the top of the cliff, all the way back to this house. It was only when he laid her down upon his bed that he realised she was a mermaid. He was so afraid, he fled not only the house, but, within a matter of weeks, the continent.

Many of our people were taken in chains by the white man, said Senhōr Gime. They were forced on to ships to cross the Atlantic. Some jumped overboard, some were pushed. Some of them became mermaids and swam back to shore.

It troubles me when I shake my pot of sand: the sound it produces is so thin. It troubles me that I decanted half of it for a stranger in Paris. The ex-boyfriend of a boyfriend wore foxes' fur to deliver the small package to the man's front door. He was older than I'd expected, the stranger, and I knew he spoke excellent French. But his long letter of thanks came in Arabic. You took it to your friend, Abdul, to translate.

It was a September morning when I found the apple. It was balancing on a five-bar gate, right in the middle of the very top rail. Its skin was so shiny and firm, it looked like it had been waxed and put there especially for me. It was the most compelling blood red – a carmine crimson I wanted to touch. I looked up and down the sunny lane, I peered into the hedge and over the gate, my eyes scanning the fields of flint on chalk. There was no one around, no one I could see. So I reached for the apple and raised it to my nose.

The perfume was immense, an outrageous temptation. All I wanted to do was bite into it and suck at the juice and feel it dribbling down my chin, but I was convinced this was some sort of trick. There, in the lane, alone but for the dog, I felt watched. Someone had set me up. They must have seen me coming from further up the hill.

I'd walked miles that day. I was hungry and tired. I'd

scored a cock pheasant on the bend in the lane where, a few days before, I'd found a deaf adder. The bird felt too warm to be dead, but when I picked it up by the claws on its feet, it swung loose and heavy like a corpse from a rope. Its wings fell open. An exuberant fan of feathers that greatly alarmed the dog.

The precise pattern of creams and silver and arrows of black on a spread of copper nudged me to contemplate, yet again, Damien Hirst's diamond-studded platinum-plated eighteenth-century skull. Fragments of conversations with artisanal diamond miners standing up to their thighs in a Kasai stream. The memory of the queue for the White Cube in Hoxton Square. The desire to know the history of each of the 8,601 stones is not yet dead, nor is the quest to track down the security guards tooled up with Uzis to protect Hirst's flash art.

And why did I lose contact with the Liberian man we met at the Hayward Gallery? The one who was on duty the day we went to see *The Alternative Guide to the Universe*, a show that might have been made just for you.

Anyway, I've kept the apple the best part of a year. At the start, it stayed in the fruit bowl that was carved to the size of a car tyre from a piece of mahogany in Indonesia. It looked ripe and robust beside the armful of dried thyme that lay on a sheet of brown paper almost weightless on the wood.

The thyme was from a garden in Romania, cut by a woman who taught me how to clean a house in two hours flat. Tricks turned by her mother, tricks that made us laugh. For years, I wondered why it was that other people's bathrooms were always so white, why the filler between their tiles was not covered in mould. What were they doing that we were not?

It was her uncle who grew the thyme. While spraying the bottom of the shower curtains with bleach, she told me about the blue roan mare that brought him home at the end of every working day, barely conscious in the back of the cart. The horse would unlock the yard gate with her teeth and top lip and pull the cart to a halt a couple of steps from the cottage front door. When the uncle sold the mare's foal to a farmer in the village next door, the horse let herself out through the same gate and went to fetch her filly. She was heard whinnying all the way there and all the way back. The police were so impressed, they refused to call it theft.

These days, the apple looks less like itself. Shrivelled and shrunk, a pink purpley brown, it reminds me more of my labia minora. Skin that is delicate, skin that is thin. Like a slice of bacon, you said, when I pushed you for a response. Like the chopped-up pieces for training the dog. The pieces that clump together and form balls inside the bag in your pocket. Pendulous, you added with a smile that became our laughter when you asked me if I always saw my labia in the objects I own.

I was lying in the bath and I told you about the growing number of girls who loathe theirs so much they want to get them chopped off. I told you about all the adult women who've already done that, and the woman in the States who turned hers into a charm on a chain. I asked you if you'd noticed the clay labia glued to the fence that runs between the riding school and the marsh land. I told you how to locate it beside the poster, Your Kindness Kills.

Snowy was a shaggy white pony whose stomach ruptured after he was fed an excess of apples by people passing by. Echoing the description of his digestive fragility, this careful sculpture of ghostly genitalia. I still catch myself imagining his collapse while wiping myself dry on the loo.

Now, the dying apple sits on a plinth that is the cork in the jar that holds the Cabindan sand. When I realised that cork and apple share the same diameter and are almost the same height, it seemed the right thing to do, to place this most intimate of things on top of this most intimate of things. Still, there are moments when I take the apple in my fingers and inhale through my nose. I try to locate the overwhelming temptation that first lured me, but it is long gone now. There was a week, maybe two, when it offered a whiff of sour fermentation, but what I smell today is so, so faint, it might not be there at all.

I can write the words of stamens and styles and sepals in pale blossom, but gazing at its sexless stalk and wrinkled flesh, my response to this apple has moved on. Its creases form crevices that are crawling from life. I see legs folded over, I see the heel of a foot, an ankle twisted and soft, and a crooked arm over the top of someone's scalp. Rotting bodies piling up.

There are tractors digging into the debris beside the river in Mosul's old town. Nothing new, says the caption in the tweet. Just more dead bodies. From my chair, it is hard to believe there are corpses in there. One image shows three bin men holding a sheet for a stretcher, but the body they carry is dead. If it is a body. The angle of the image reveals what looks like a pile of junk. I need to see the bones of a hand to be convinced.

I return to my apple. It demands to be studied. Why on earth have I kept it all this time? I think I thought I'd show it to you and, if you thought it was safe, we'd eat it. I wanted to watch you slicing it open with one of the two Swiss Army knives we were given with our names in italics engraved into the blade. But by the time I returned home, it was already too late. Its skin no longer shone and my suspicions had grown. The gate on which I'd found it opens into a field that belongs to that man, the one who waited for you outside the church to tell you he'd met and admired Colonel Gaddafi, and could he meet your wife?

Two weeks later, I was ushered into an eighteenth-century house off London's Park Lane by a short man from Manila who wore a bowler hat. From the hall, I was led to the library by a woman from the Cotswolds. Her neck was loose white fat and she wore an old-fashioned bra and smelt of lavender talc. The men sitting inside said they liked my suede boots. They asked me what I drink. They said they needed someone like me, they offered me bottles of wine. They wanted to know about English football teams and puppies, and who eats Edam cheese.

I can't help it. When I look at the desiccated apple stalk, what I see is something resembling my clitoral hood when I am dead. Still, there are so many wrinkles in my apple's skin, every day is another battle for space. They come in at perpendicular angles, always thrusting and on the attack. I turn the fruit in my fingers and roll it around my palm. I'm searching for that face Frank Auerbach drew in charcoal and chalk – the bold black marks, the firm short lines that either hold the light or shun the light and insist on a female form.

Instead, Babi Yar comes back into my mind. Translated from the Ukrainian, so I've been told, Babi Yar almost means old woman's ravine. And now I can't seem to untangle my thoughts about my body from the images I have seen of this mass grave. I trawl through the internet, wanting to find out more. Long before it was deliberately flooded and filled with rubbish, then levelled and covered up, it was two and a half kilometres long and fifty metres deep. Before the war, it had been a weekend picnic spot, a place where families would go to splash in the stream at the bottom of the ravine, to sunbathe and relax.

It was that same September, during the days when I found the dead pheasant and the deaf adder and the poison apple, that I began to use an electric current to stop the dog from chasing deer. Like a handgun delivered for a mission, the equipment arrived in a heavy black case. It was immediate, the recognition within myself of a certain manliness. You noticed, too. You said something about our shared pool of masculine and feminine. You said that you become more female when I become more male.

I knew I was in charge when my thumbs released the flat locks either side of the handle. The lid sprung open and my chest smiled at the arrangement of slick black tools laid out before me. The stiffness of the collar, and the receiver, solid as a lifeboat, were particularly pleasing. I was reassured by the explicit seriousness of the brass contact points, upright and ready to enter the zone, like pawns at the start of a game of chess. I was surprised by my impulse to press them into my neck, to imagine Dracula had come to suck me. How spectacular, the sensation of cold metal entering the jugular! Even the black metal tongue, which I screwed to the back of the transmitter in order to clip it to my belt, had obviously been designed with militarism in mind. Sliding it on to the leather at my waist, I caught myself wishing it was a gun returning to its holster. If I had looked down at that very moment and witnessed my surging manhood, I would have laughed. Now, I own you all!

And yet, the experience of unwrapping this equipment – equipment which I had rejected for so long – was complicated. When I placed the collar on the table, the light that shone through three dozen buckle holes softened the shadow on the curve and I looked at the moon. When I unwrapped the tiny, transparent test light from its excess of tape and bubble wrap, I took it in my fingers and held it beneath my abdomen, pressing it into the zip of my jeans and closing my eyes. It's hard to believe there's a uterus in there, just as it is hard to believe in a spleen. The test light looks like a contraceptive device. Something to be wedged in a womb.

In fact, the first time I tested the collar, I strapped it around my father's arm. Nice and tight, with the contact points pushing into the pale and papery flesh of his octogenarian biceps, close to the basilic vein. We began at level five. I pressed the button: he felt nothing. We progressed to ten. I pressed the button: still, he felt nothing. I tried fifteen: again, nothing. At twenty, he smiled. A wren's peck, he said. At twenty-five, his smile expanded and I began to laugh. A crow, he said. At thirty, he blew out air. Shall I stop? I asked. He shook his head, he seemed to be enjoying it. At thirty-three, more air. At thirty-eight, he winced and I laughed some more. At forty-four, we were both laughing so much, he bounced in his chair. At fifty, he asked me to stop.

That night my father collapsed.

There are days when I want to embody the qualities of a thing. To be effective, but not affected. To be present, but not involved. When I told you that I envy certain objects, you told me about the okapi, a relative of the giraffe that looks like a zebra. It lives a life in solitude in the forests in the north-east of the DRC. Not long after giving birth, the female okapi leaves her young alone for many days while she goes in search of food. The calf, which is born with false eyelashes, remains completely still until the adult returns. It doesn't even defecate.

Sometimes I catch myself longing to be like you. To be a man sitting in silence. Like the corner of the bed frame when I bump into it in the dark in the middle of the night on my way to wee. I shout and curse, and the pain in my shin causes havoc in my head, but the bed does nothing. Dark shape, down there, unmoved. It does not breathe, and I hate it for throwing me back upon myself.

Even the hairbrush has its moments. The hairbrush that I like to hold like a table-tennis bat, which is to say back to front. I like to be ready for the young man from Tokushima, who is sweating and lively and out of my league. He bats the ball back and I crouch beside the sink to swallow my laughs.

I rarely look in the mirror, even when brushing my hair. I prefer to bend over and bounce through my hips until I can press my forehead into these granular kneecaps. I like feeling the skin on my shins tightening at the touch of my locks hanging long and loose. My hair swaying heavy and wise like the weeping willow on the east side of Stamford Hill where old Tony sucks fat cigars and waits patiently for the Hasidic Jew from Cameroon. Doubled down here, blood flushing my face, the room is topsy-turvy and I am briefly young. I rest the hairbrush on the back of my neck. I let its bristles roll over my scalp, and I brush and I brush until my hair is a bonfire of static. That smell of an old bachelor's flat. Nothing quite dirty, nothing quite clean. Traces of evening meals swallowed in solace with Claude Debussy among dusty succulents and stale crumbs and empty tins that never made it to the tap.

In the Boots queue, I was hopeful. Standing there, waiting my turn, I reacquainted myself with memories of being held between adult thighs to endure the peculiar agony that grabs the back of the throat when bristles yank at a clump of hair clinging to the scalp. The untangling of schizotrichia.

I felt certain, inside the mall, beneath the anaemic light, that this hairbrush would accompany me to my death. This lightweight wood, so at home in my hand, allowing me to see myself as the middle-aged woman I know I've become. Like a briefcase or a Filofax or a tray of tea on a blanketed bed, its rectangular shape at once comforting and dull. Were it not for the tiny nests at the base of every bristle, I might have spiralled into bitter loathing long ago. As it is, I have embraced these perfect spheres of twisted hair, and the flakes of skin caught in the softest, palest fluff. As if we aren't all desperate enough! Plucking these cosy cocoons gives me almost as much pleasure as the afternoon I held the astonishingly industrious creation of a long flown, long gone blackbird in the bush. Broken twigs and threads and plastic and mud. So light, I felt I might float.

As for my hair, there are days when I can hardly believe it grows from my head. One particular handful rolls around like the clump of desert grass you filmed on the edge of the Sahara shortly before we watched that young, male camel crumple to the ground, his legs tied together, his scrotum slit wide. The way they pulled out all the gooey white stuff, twisting and stretching it, the camel howling with regret.

I will always respect my hair's reluctance to relinquish the brush. The more my fingers pull, the more elongated it becomes, the individual hairs forming a structure like a cat's cradle that stretches into something resembling the loofah in the bathroom in the old corner shop I shared before I knew you. Thinking back to those days, dribble dresses my lower lip. I can taste plantain fried in butter and brown sugar, and dusted with powdered cinnamon. I can smell spiced bread browning on a grill. I can see a room on Brixton Hill. A young woman is spinning on a Catherine's wheel while her boyfriend pulls on his cock.

When the hair finally comes free, I am holding a thing of magic. A perfect sphere of hazel and silvered curls, indifferent to my touch. Yet, here, in the palm of my hand, I sense, fleetingly, a spirit touching down on the skin. Because it is more like a sculpture, because it is so reassuringly round, I want to hang it from invisible thread inside something old-fashioned, something antique, some structure made from glass. I want to study it until it triggers memories of weavers' woven nests and astronomical objects and walking under the pergola in the rose garden at Hyde Park, those thorny climbers twisting around metal spines and falling in abundance from the dome above our heads.

That was the day the gravel path gave us so much comfort. Our feet felt firm following the track towards The Serpentine, where we met that young man who seemed to hold half the world in his eyes. He smiled at the little rowing boats moving steadily across the water. The sun shone and he told us that the last time he'd seen boats like these, he was inside one. He told us about his younger brother, still in Calais inside a camp. He's waiting for happiness, he said.

He showed us how he'd squeezed himself into a metal structure, which he described as one might a dog cage, conveniently fixed to the underside of the articulated lorry that carried him from Rome to Paris. We were sitting on a bench beside the lake when he stood up and immediately collapsed into himself, like one of those tents people take to festivals and abandon when they leave. Folded flat, he slotted his body beneath the slats of our seat. You and I looked at each other awkwardly as we listened to him breathing hard against the tarmac only inches from our thighs. He wasn't a big man. Even so, we were impressed at the speed and ease at which he inserted himself down there.

Afterwards, when he was sitting back between us again, I asked him questions about his journey. He said his father had been shot dead at a wedding. His mother had managed to run away, but he's never seen or spoken to her since. After a long silence he said, She might be in Pakistan. Then he looked at you and thanked you for listening. He called you Sir and you blushed and you told him your name. By the time we parted, it felt as if we had all known each other some considerable length of time.

You took my hand – do you remember? – and we watched him walking east along the north side of the water. Neither of us spoke until he had peeled off towards Marble Arch, a lively figure narrowing out of sight. I couldn't resist reminding you that the last time we'd sat together beside this body of water we were waiting for your ex-wife. She was staying in some hotel on the north side of the park with her new beau. I remember trying to disguise my surprise when I noticed this short woman waving her arms and shouting your name. She wore a spectacularly high pair of heels and her dress was a silk square a little longer than her hair. On your suggestion, the four of us took a boat out onto the lake.

While you rowed, I gazed at the gusset of her knickers and found myself thinking about you in ways I might never have imagined. She told us about their house in California, about the garden with its hot tub. She spoke excitedly about all the friends who come to skinny-dip.

Of course, you two are invited! she said. We go buck!

She was smiling at me, goading me, and I looked at you. I was listening to the sound of the oars in the water and watching you watching the blades. I was so caught up in the bundle of my thoughts, I didn't notice the conversation switch to Israel. She never thanked you for what you did.

I've started collecting the dog's hair too. It seemed such a waste, watching it blow away, free as the breeze, until it got caught in the ivy or trapped in the spiders' webs that cling to the old brick wall, clogged up, dirty and wet.

I won't disagree: it is quite a ceremony. When I brush the side of his long white neck, he flops to the floor, legs extending, front and back, like a horse on a merry-go-round with a pole of cast aluminium pierced through its spine. His eyes close, his lashes flutter, his lower jaw begins to tremble. An orgasm, you remarked, leaning from the kitchen window, and you smiled at me and the dog.

I have continued grooming him into bliss, improving my technique with the metal comb in one hand and a gentleman's beard brush with bristles of wild boar hair in the other.

When I told the man with the Jackapoo that I'd bought my dog a hairbrush in Pak's, he asked me whether I was aware that it was at a branch of Pak's that several hundred litres of hydrogen peroxide had been bought as part of a failed bomb plot. I tried to engage him by telling him that I've collected just over four ounces of soft silver fur. You need at least six for a decent pair of socks, I said, which is the weight of a reliable lightweight hand grenade. I continued along this thread, explaining how much I'd learned about wool – that it should never be kept in an air-tight container or a plastic bag, that it needs to breathe even though it is dead. I told him that I keep my dog's hair in an organic cotton pouch under the stairs and that it reminds me of a bag of candy floss, and that this always makes me salivate. I want to scoop it up, soft and impacted, and hold it on my tongue. I want to make it crunch like broken asbestos. I want to make it melt inside my mouth.

When I told the woman in the wool shop that I was collecting my dog's hair, her whole face seemed to fold in on itself. It's only wool when it comes from sheep, she said. The rest is yarn. I wish I'd had the wit to contradict her, to explain that dog's hair, when spun, is not yarn. It's chiengora. But I only discovered this later in the day when I borrowed your phone.

I've also learned that dog hair is eight times warmer than sheep's because the individual strands of dog hair are hollow. I know this because I've spent several afternoons browsing specialist websites created by a community of mainly heterosexual, apparently retired couples who own long-haired hounds and also knit. There are pages and pages of portraits of noble dogs standing beside their owners, who are all wearing large fluffy jumpers made from their dear dogs' coats. I would quite like to be on the fringes of this club. I would probably start with something small. A pair of mittens does excite me, or a stylish bobble hat.

I had hoped that the woman in the wool shop might be able to help, but when I raised the matter she quickly bustled me towards the door.

The little girl who came to dinner showed more commitment. She lowered her face into my bag of dog hair and drew several long breaths through her nose. It smells like vomit, she said, and she slid from her chair and began dancing, pointing her toes and leaping from side to side. You're like a happy frog, you told her, and she lifted her skirt in her little webbed fingers and pranced and hopped in circles. Shortly, her father told her to sit down, so she planted herself on a chair and made a series of statements about books and pets.

She asked you for more of the tiny silver balls that we'd scattered on top of the cake, and you poured some into her cupped hands. She talked about how happy she feels when her grandmother washes her hair once a week. My skin unrolls down my spine, she said, and she yelped in sheared delight. You were so impressed by this sentence that your smile expanded into your cheeks and your eyelashes thickened and shone. But the little girl's grandmother tutted and sighed. She slapped the girl hard on the wrist.

I told the old woman about your corkscrew locks, how I wish I could have touched them and turned them into yarn and worn your hair upon my feet. I would like to be able to follow the path into his past, I said. When she replied she wouldn't look me in the eye. She seemed to suck the words in as soon as she spoke them.

I know a tale or two about human hair, she said, but not now, not here, not in front of the child.

In a ceramic pot the size of an adult eyeball, I keep a tiny hand. I found it while I was looking at my feet while I was examining the tarmac that replaced the grass verge. I keep a tiny wooden shopping basket, too. It belongs to the elasticated lady who collapses to a curtsey when you push the button inside the cylindrical plinth on which she stands. I've also got three of the dog's puppy teeth – two canines and a pre-molar – and the entire nail from my left big toe, which finally fell off at the end of a run.

It had been flapping like a forgotten window and making bubbles in the bath. Drying it carefully with the corner of a towel, I couldn't resist squeezing it, to hear it sucking like lime jelly spooned from a Pyrex bowl. I had thought to say that it sounded like wet labia on a walk, but I wasn't sure you'd believe me. I also thought to say it sounded like sex, like licking lips and curling tongues and slimy genitalia, but it probably wasn't quite that loud. It's only a toenail after all.

At dinner, when I held up this crusty curl of alpha-keratin, you recoiled. You told me to put it away. Later, in bed, you said it reminded you of the windscreen from your Airfix Space Shuttle kit. A piece of parmesan, I replied. I want to put it in my mouth, and bite it and lick it and touch it with my tongue. Instead, I've given it to the tiny hand to hold. I've wedged it between its white fingers and thumb, and glued that to the top of my computer screen. Now, it's a dirty handkerchief waving tears and dread at a chartered flight that is waiting to take to the air.

Two other nails I have kept include the one from your big toe. Its deep maroon reminds me of the Rothko chapel and the Victoria plums begging to be plucked from the branches draped over the Tottenham canal. I thought it was a hawk moth, the day you left it on the rug. I lowered my hand with so much care to the floor. I waited for it to flap.

I've also kept the nail from my little finger because it's

the same shape as the kites that the surfers hang on to, in the wind, on Constantine Bay. I will never forget the time I saw that man scooting up the most enormous wave and flying off the top of it as if he were leaping a row of terraced houses. Up there in the dunes, I was whooping and shouting and racing the gale. I hoped he would never come down.

What is it about flesh that falls off? Why do I get so much pleasure feeling in my fingers a bit of broken body? Why such a singular thrill when I tuck a piece away, when I slip it somewhere safe? Am I hoping it will come back to life? Do I believe there's something alive in there, some sort of knowledge that stays with the body no matter how many bits it becomes?

Like the crow's head I found in the forest. A tidy decapitation lying alone on the narrow path. It was so smooth and glossy, I couldn't help but stroke its crown and its long, soft cheek. There were no wings, no tail, no random feathers from a fight. Just a head and a neck and a big black beak.

Admiring this perfection, I examined its face and looked into its eyes. I felt I knew this bird and that it knew me. I was waiting for its words, for its scarecrow stories, for all the secrets it would share with me. So I picked it up and slipped it into my pocket. I brought it home to boil and clean.

Sometimes I speak to my wooden stool, but my wooden stool does not speak back. Within its bulging belly and each one of its dependable legs, it holds every word I spoke the day I acquired it. It knows that I laughed and jested, that I was proud to have argued in another language and won. It knows that I claimed it as my own, but that it is no more mine now than when it was the blemished trunk of a tree. It remembers the answers demanded by my friend as we walked away from the trader and his stall. How could you do that? How's the guy supposed to eat?

He went on and on, even after we'd found the colonial golf course and were lying on the hot sand of the estuary and I experienced déjà vu. Even when I discovered that the stool was designed to hold tusks – when I'd turned it upside down and noticed the holes either side of its trunk – still, he would not give up. If only he knew, after all these years, that every time I look at this block of wood I think of him and what he said and I ask myself, Why did you buy this ten-inch elephant with a circular seat carved out of its back?

I try to forget that I haggled so hard for something I didn't much like. I try not to remember what it was I wanted and why I wanted to bring it back home. I try not to think about elephants' tusks hacked from heads and the ivory rings I bought the same day. I try not to obsess about this stool, which I know will never miss me. I won't even be the memory that is vague. Disinterest seeps from its dead weight.

Yet, still this stool stirs strange loyalties. Long before I held you, I held it. Long before I sat on you, I sat upon it, the bones in my buttocks, a catamaran on wood. With my heels to its trunk, with my chin upon my knees, I see the district nurse spread wide as a marquee in the carpeted corridor that leads to the loo. They should be built lower to facilitate defecation, she said. The trouble with most toilets is they're far too high, which is why so many people strain and end up with piles. What you want is a hole in the ground, she said. What you want is a jolly good squat.

There is an inspiring squat in *Les Demoiselles d'Avignon*. Five naked women in peach pale pink. Larger than life size, they fill the canvas square. Four are standing. Arms stretched up or over, hands reaching behind necks, maybe down to a shoulder. One squats. She has her back to us, head and neck twisting left. Over her shoulder, she stares back. In the words of Picasso's most devoted biographer, it is the tribalisation of her head, and that of the other woman on the right of the painting, that is the most striking feature.

I feel bewildered by the idea of a tribalised head, but I appreciate the assertion that this development in abstraction in Picasso's work owes everything to the African masks he saw at the Ethnographical Museum in Paris. For years, and despite myriad sketches strongly suggesting otherwise, the Spaniard denied that outstanding sculptures from the African continent had inspired his 1907 masterpiece.

In 1920, in response to a journalist's question, he said: African art? Never heard of it.

I'm less interested in his deceit than the fifth woman's squat. Her knees are so far apart, her buttocks so close to the ground, it is astonishing to think of her holding this pose long enough to be photographed, let alone sketched, in a dark Parisian room.

I have tried to emulate the demoiselle in the study for squatting, which Picasso drew in black ink some eight years after *Heart of Darkness* was published in three parts. To say that I am hopeless is true. Whereas she has both feet flat on the floor, my heels hover. Whereas her back is perpendicular and proud, mine curls forward, wrestling with gravity and muscles too tight. Whereas her hands rest elegant and firm over her strong splayed thighs, mine reach for the door handle, or the lip of the desk, or the wide collar around the dog's neck. Whereas her head is lifted, her chin throwing up space for the neck, mine sinks into rings of loose flesh. My mouth grimaces, my eyes scrunch. I salute Fernande Olivier, the model and mistress who Picasso described as a whore.

From time to time, I still like to try the squat taught me by a Zimbabwean friend. It is the squat taught her by her grandmother over a purpose-built ditch, which she was told to straddle, her small feet either side. Standing up, squatting down, standing up, squatting down, over and over, holding the position for longer and longer, lower and lower, feet a good foot apart.

I look at my stool. It is silent on sex. No notes on technique. At seventeen, I knew more about holding a car on a corner – slowly in, quickly out – than pinning another body to a bed. I can't have been more than twelve when I learned how to make a Victoria sponge rise and how to ensure it stayed up when pulled from the oven. I never imagined holding a stiff cock. I never imagined, the first time I did, that it would feel so familiar, it would be like holding the handle of my hairbrush. Lying there beside that naked male body, secretly, privately, brushing my hair.

The mask I bought you looks like Wallace, not Gromit, and I bought it because it looks like you too. I bought it beside the Atlantic, on a bench on a beach with sand so soft I wanted to lie down and sleep. It was carved by a sculptor whose name I do not know. It was transported on a bus from the border with the DRC. It is not a big mask, not a heavy mask. Its wooden form fits so neatly on to my left hand, it might have been made to measure. And I have measured it. It is nineteen centimetres long and ten and a half centimetres wide, which is the same length as my hand and the same width as your right foot.

What is this obsession with numbers, this desire to gather facts? When did it first occur to Bruno Berger to measure, with metal calipers, the size of someone's head?

When I look at this mask, I see your bald head. I see your high forehead and your slim, arched eyebrows. I see your thin lips and your trim, tidy teeth. I see your mouth, which, when you smile, seems to stretch the entire width of your jaw, trying to touch your lobes. I see your long, fine nose and your high cheek bones. I see your soft eyes closing and I close mine to Achebe's words on Conrad: Travellers with closed minds can tell us little except about themselves.

When I look at this mask, I think of the woman I met in Chicago. She worked for months in Chokwe territory. When I asked her for her thoughts on Europeans who hang African masks inside their homes, she told me about the time she'd been invited to an estate auction in Illinois. Several pieces of Chokwe art were among the items for sale. In fact the catalogue was so tempting, she decided to take the trip. She arrived good and early and wandered through every room. She marked down the pieces she liked, and was on the verge of making a bid when the ceiling in the room collapsed. An omen, she said. She fled.

When I gave you the mask, you asked whether it was fake or real and I told you about the calculator I was given when I turned eight. Receiving that machine seemed to offer the certainty that I had a good brain. It seemed to say to the little girl who unwrapped it, You are smart. So when she tipped it out of its box onto her lap, it took several drawn-out seconds before she realised that what she had been given was, in fact, a bar of soap. It shared the shape of the calculator captured in colour on its cardboard container, but it was pink and perfume-free. It flaked under the nail. In that moment, I wished more than ever before that I had been born a boy.

The size of a small blood orange, the Wedgwood trinket pot that I was given on the same birthday as the soap was disconcerting, too. What to do with it? Fill it with unconvincing jewellery, like those gold horseshoe earrings I was given (as if I needed luck)? Something about that Jasper matt blue sitting still on a white gloss mantelpiece insisting I obey.

Here I am, lying on my back, legs spread wide on a pale blue sheet, some unknown beast, curled horns and razor tail, humping away, panting at my ribs. Here I am in a pale blue room, legs spread wide, gripping and pushing and panting and splitting and, at last, giving birth to wet life. Here I am, in a pale blue chair, breastfeeding the sticky bundle, nipples cracking open pain, exhausted and washed out and stale and spent.

In this piece of Wedgwood, I detected the demand for a kidney-shaped dressing table at which I should sit, day after day, my bare legs gone goose-bump against the cold curtained skirt. Instead of gaining inspiration from its neoclassical decoration – its border of berries and laurel leaves, its winged white stallion – I couldn't bear to be anywhere near it. Simply allowing my gaze to rest briefly upon its crisp chalky surface was enough to fill me with dread. Drawn into the future by this piece of pottery, which I knew could never reach out and touch me, produced as much anxiety as the spectre of forced marriage. I can still remember how much I feared lifting its lid, convinced that one day it was going to grab my fingers, clamp them hard and harder, until they burst and bled.

When I press one of my fingers into the soft, spongy teat that barely protrudes from the plastic casing of the thermostat, I am calm. These buttons, so small and unobtrusive, so pleasing to touch, like velvet merged with rubber, like the tip of the tragus at the front of your ear. Shouldn't they be awkward and ugly and heavy to lift? Shouldn't they be so hard to handle that every time you think to turn up the temperature, you must consider whether it is worth cranking your body out of the sofa and staggering towards the machinery in the hallway to wrestle with a lever that is rusting and stiff? Shouldn't the handle be covered in slime composed of the sweat and the spit, the bogey and shit collected from the bodies of those who scoop up the profits from the fossil fuel firms they control? Shouldn't these excretions include a droplet of Vladimir Putin's palest semen diluted with a dribble of Donald Trump's, a squirt of Mohammed bin Salman Al Saud's? And if you dare turn up your heating, if you accept the invitation on the flip-down flap to Change Desired Temperature, shouldn't the stink of this substance stay inside you for long days and deprived nights, no matter how vigorously you scrub your hands with mechanics' soap and Brillo pad, no matter how often you gargle TCP?

My blue burner phone is worse. Strangers see me with my bar of plastic and they smile as they might at the sight of a miserable child pushing a doll in a pram. Occasionally, there's the joke about dealers. It's never funny, but sometimes you laugh at me being laughed at and sometimes I laugh too.

Most of the time, this handy little gadget is so determinedly unimportant, so lacking in weight, I often forget it's here at all. Even when I place it inside the dedicated slot of my running tights, a slippy stretch of Lycra separating its smooth surface from the blotched skin that covers my quads, it succeeds in distilling itself. My blue burner and its marvellous vanishing trick.

Its predecessor was orange. Whenever I took the time to look at it properly, to study it as I might a painting, my mouth would fill with those brittle bubbles that come from sucking orange-flavoured vitamin C tablets the size of antique blazer buttons.

Last summer, I dropped it while walking along a country lane. It slipped from the top pocket of your old red mac as I bent over to pick up a stick abandoned by the dog. It surprised me, the speed at which it spun across the cracked tarmac into the nettles and damp cow parsley beside the ditch. I found the SIM card and the back plastic casing soon enough, but the main body of the phone and its flat black battery were nowhere to be seen. Crouching down, peering into the base of the hedge, I felt myself transforming into an obscure mass. On the other side, a pheasant screamed the alarm. When I stood up, it erupted into flight, the tall flame of a gas flare.

Walking along that lane, I tried to remember the name of the town in southern Congo, the one where toddlers cut cobalt from rock, where exposure to toxic heavy metals is leading to stillbirths and foetal abnormalities, where babies are born with legs that won't unfold and girls as young as one have been raped by men who believe that sex with a virgin will increase their chances of finding cobalt under the ground and decrease the chance of death. I tried to work out the difference between myself with my mobile phone and the millions of men who, in their desperate attempts to be sexually aroused, pay to download images of children being abused.

The truth is, I've even noticed a feeling of excitement creeping up on me when I'm holding my mobile phone inside my pocket. It's the gratitude that comes from the knowledge that, here I am, walking around with a tiny piece of Congo in my hand, as if it could make up for all the Englishness I loathe. Here I am with my mobile phone calling you to tell you that I've just been eating wild black-berries the size of plums beside the Kingsmill factory, that I am watching a young fox dozing in the grass on the edge of the forest, that the pale man with thin spectacles and three fat dogs has just tried to put his tongue inside my mouth on the path that runs beneath the railway bridge, that I've just seen another grass snake in the ditch beside London's last unploughed field, that a man in a purple turban is bowling cricket balls for his nine-year-old daughter and she's whacking them into space, that I was eavesdropping on a pair of Brazilian women who were laughing uncontrollably while sharing details of the large houses they clean near Mornington Crescent, that the dog just caught a young, violet pigeon and I'd had to finish it off with my own hands in front of a male cyclist who seemed unfamiliar with death, that I never knew Babak's brother had become addicted to opium aged twelve, that I've met a man who has told me how to deflate the tyres of an SUV without using a knife and will you do it with me?, that I've reached a truce with the guy who keeps leaving half-drunk bottles of brandy on the kerb beside our house, that I've apologised for the bucket of water I threw at his friend, that I want to travel to Guinea Bissau before it's too late, that Nina Simone is changing the quality of my intellectual and emotional life, that she was a genius, that I can't believe I didn't understand this earlier in life, that visiting Edinburgh allowed me to experience the lightness of living in a land that won't vote Tory, that I think I want to become a backing singer, part of a trio, swaying and swinging and clicking our fingers in rhythm in harmony in tight blue jeans, that I've realised I am definitely, whole-heartedly, entirely anti-capitalist and I'm thankful for that, that I've never been certain of what it means to be a woman, that I prefer wooden clogs to new-born babies, that before we're too old I want you and I to take LSD in a skateboard park, that I have so much rage for the government I'm beginning to wonder if it's actually a superpower, that I'm concerned my skill set is limited to topiary, that I've just been pinned down by evangelising Christians for the second time in a month, that I'm not sure for how much longer I can continue to avoid flying because I'm missing certain people so much my heart aches, that I'm sorry I got cross about the ladder to the attic and, yes, you're right, it doesn't matter anyway, that this is just a message to remind you to rub some of that Elizabeth Arden Eight Hour Cream my mother gave us for the dog's paws into your elbow, that I've been wondering where all the spiders are this year, the ones that spin those enormous webs between the washing line and the ceanothus, that I just heard a crow saying Oh my God! Oh my God! as it flew overhead, that I wish you were with me to hear the man playing his saxophone beneath the grey poplars, serenading the streams of parakeets returning to roost in the branches above the Lea, that I don't know what to do to try to save life on this planet, that I know you've only been gone since breakfast but I'm already missing you, that you forgot your lunch, that I really like all the bin men who work our street, that I think my diarrhoea is finally clearing up, that the dog just twisted his ankle chasing a crow on the football field so we will be slow in getting home, that I forgot to mention the butcher – could you ask him if he sells tripe, that the amplifier is quietly screaming and I can't stop it, that I'm beginning to wish I believed in a God and could we discuss this tonight, that

I've eaten all the chocolate again and I wish you wouldn't buy it, that I regret not coming to Julius Eastman before now and I'm grateful to Oto for showing me the way, that I wish I could own an Auerbach oil – even a very small one that I could gaze into whenever I wished, that yes, you're right, I do live life with my emotional choke pulled out, that the little boy who I sprayed with water while he ran around the garden without any clothes on has just asked me if your purple toenail is still purple, that the menopause has got me thinking that perhaps women really are the weaker sex and I don't think I can bear much more of this, that I've just seen a man with a face that might have been sculpted from wax sprinting into Chico's café shouting He's going to stab me! Hide me!, that I've just had a curious conversation with a pale man who told me that his tidy dog in a close-fitting harness has two or three panic attacks a day because it suffers from some form of PTSD not brought on by anything in particular, whereas his brother, who was seventeen when he was sent to fight in Angola, has suffered from PTSD for thirty-eight years, that I'd like to buy this eyelash curler but I wish it didn't remind me quite so much of the stainless-steel speculum that was wedged into my vagina by a nervous medical student at my first smear test, that I keep thinking about what that man said – that people burn very well, that the dog's just caught a squirrel and it's quite a large one so you don't need to worry about supper, that I'm about to get on the bus, that no one's wearing a mask, that I might walk, that I offered to share the squirrel with the neighbours via the street WhatsApp group and someone's now left the group, that there's an armed raid going down at number fifty-five and the brothers are in their boxers being cuffed and I've just asked the older one if he's OK and he said he's fine thanks, that of course I will meet you at the tube, that I love you, that I'm missing you, that I can't wait to come home.

To come home to our front door and take hold of the elegant brass handle, which sparks up old fantasies of a galloping thoroughbred pulling down on an eggbutt snaffle. Such a wholesome pair of words! There was a time when I was saying eggbutt snaffle several days a week. I think life was simpler back then. I should probably say eggbutt snaffle more often.

Eggbutt snaffle,

eggbutt snaffle,

eggbutt snaffle,

eggbutt snaffle.

I bought the brass handle from the ironmonger because he said it would be like holding the waxing crescent of the moon. He wrapped it in a page torn from a tabloid. Oh, pleasure! Watching his pale, jocular hands make little tucks and long folds as he rolled news from Kabul around seven brass hooks, a report about Cooper the Rottweiler getting stuck on the roof of a 1930s holiday home in

Ilfracombe around a dozen fifty-mil screws, and a feature about how to grow your glutes around a pair of six-inch cast-iron brackets. The possibilities are endless.

Sometimes, he even lets me choose the page. Even so, I'm always disappointed when I return home, when I'm standing in the kitchen, unwrapping one of his parcels, not to find a forfeit written on a strip of foolscap between the layers of news. How can he resist? He must know the game. He must have played it at parties when he was a kid. Surely he will succumb, sooner or later? I have wondered if I shouldn't work at the shop myself. I'd be happy to write forfeits all day long, and I'd slip in boiled sweets and Animal Bars, transfers and fleeting tattoos. I'd make cups of lukewarm tea and hold a pencil with my ear.

Oh, eggbutt snaffle! There are evenings when I come home and I grab that handle and I hear his voice so clearly, his east London lilt producing three-note harmonies as he's totting up down a margin in *The Mirror*. There are evenings when I've caught myself wondering if a part of him is held inside the curve of the brass.

I'll be standing there, key in hand, thinking about his clothes and wondering whether, in the old days, in the days when The Baker's Arms really was The Baker's Arms, not a gambling shop, he ever wore a khaki warehouse coat. Thinking about his other life as a free jazz musician playing harmonica, occasionally drums. Thinking about the hundreds of tiny wooden coffers that contain every size of screw in every kind of material, every pin and nail you could ever need, every type of drawer handle, every hinge and lock, every key, every washer, every plug and bolt, every turnbuckle, every nut and hook, every hook and eye, every lifting loop, every ratchet and ratchet tensioner, every doorstop, every curtain pole ring and every curtain hook, every dowel, every letter box, every ball-bearing, every thimble, every knocker, every screwdriver, and every size of chain.

All of this and all of the old man's knowledge, all the years he has run the shop, all the advice he has offered, all the orders he has made, all the care that has gone into the design of his store, all his anxieties and all of his joys. All of this is held inside my brass handle, such that, every time I touch this slender piece of metal, I feel the love for his labour, the love passed down from his dad and on to his sons.

I feel their bond and I feel blessed.


Will you keep reading if I tell you about the broom? The fat, sturdy one with stiff red bristles sprouting from its head like a crop of wholewheat spaghetti. Normally, it hangs from the pipe above the outdoor toilet, but I've brought it indoors so I can stare at it, unafraid.

The first time I saw it, it was hooked up beside bowsaws

the size of pigs. The way it looked back at me, I sensed we'd met before, I can't think where, but I'm pretty sure the old man noticed because he only charged me ten quid. God, I was proud carrying it out of the shop. We were untouchable, my broom and me! More like, me and my RPG, the way I balanced it, stylishly, on my clavicle. I wanted to spin in circles, faster and faster, swinging it round and round, until, sick and dizzy, I would fall to the ground, my broom in my arms. I wanted to smash it into other things too, like traffic lights and fully stacked supermarket shelves, and the waxed bonnets of SUVs.

The Norwegian gamekeeper told me that the quickest way to kill a small mammal is to grab it by the hind legs and swing it down on to the top rail of a fence or hurl it at a tree trunk. If you do it hard enough, he said, you break the animal's back. We were standing on a pleasant amount of gravel a couple of feet from a chatty family, who were sitting at a table eating bits of meat. In fact, all around us were eating people, a disproportionate number of them either grandparents or babies. It felt staged. Some of them kept distracting the gamekeeper by calling out his name, which I couldn't determine, or blowing their whistles. A man in a yellow lambswool tank-top beckoned us to join his table, but the gamekeeper tapped the hairs on the back of his hand and nodded his head at my jaw.

I wanted to tell him about Armando, the older Andalusian I met in the nineties in Granada, in the Albaicín. The spitting image of Derek Walcott minus the moustache. He'd fought in the civil war and remained a proud Francoist with only one regret. He'd watched his group commander take a child by the ankles and swing her, like an axe, at the trunk of a tree. Again and again, until she was dead. Armando was seventeen years old. He was a soldier. He was ordered to hold the child's mother. He was ordered to make her watch.

When *White Egrets* came out in 2010, I finally relaxed into poetry. Every line in that slim blue book made sense. I mean, utterly. Every page flung open its arms. I wanted to write to Walcott to thank him with all my heart, but every word seemed weak. So I wrote to his lookalike instead, hoping he was still alive.

As well as my letter, I enclosed a copy of the book. I urged him to turn straight to page 25, to 'Spanish Series', to the end of verse II:

> Your lashes like black moths, like twigs your frail
>     wrists,
> your small, cynical mouth with its turned-down
>     answer,
> when it laughs, is like a soft stanza
> in a ballad by Lorca, your teeth are white stones
> in a river-bed, I hear the snorting stallions
> of Córdoba in heat, I hear my bones'
> castanets, and a rattle of heels like machine guns.

You are one of the snorting stallions of Córdoba, I told

Armando before asking him if he had known that the civil guards who dragged Federico García Lorca from his home in Granada in the August heat had been ordered to give him coffee, lots of coffee. I told him that the Nazis spoke of coffee vans when referring to their killing trucks. I asked him, Why coffee?

I caught myself reflecting on Armando's face while I was out on the street with my broom. I was sweeping up golden leaves like giant cornflakes and I was thinking about all the incarcerated men in Libya who have been ordered to rape each other with broom handles. It was described in detail in a report I read, and I will keep imagining their pain. Some of these prisoners have been forced to lower themselves on to the end of a broom that is fixed to a wall. Guards point guns at them and shout orders to push harder so that the handle goes deeper. They are only allowed to stop when blood can be seen on the pole.

I was confused when my father spoke of the man who'd arrived in A&E with a broom handle stuck inside his rectum. He told the nurse he'd fallen down the stairs. He said he'd landed on the broom. Another time, my father told us about a man who couldn't release a milk bottle from his anus because his sphincter muscles had gone into spasm. In those days, milk bottles were shaped like rockets flying into space.

Perhaps this is why I like my broom. It embodies force. It is a good weight, a weight you have to take seriously.

In the wrong hands, it is unwieldy. It stands on its head, bouncing on bristles as tough as knuckledusters. And yet, it always persuades me to be kind. I end up sweeping not only the brick path in our back garden – and the York stone that the builder gave us after a client decided it wasn't quite the right shade for her clematis, apparently a Jewel of Merk – but the neighbour's front garden too, and the entire top end of our street. I get carried away pulling up weeds in front of other people's houses, clearing the roadside gutters and sweeping up the sludge of leaves rotting in a pile-up above another blocked drain.

This summer, I went further. I swept half the next street too. We were a small group with a lot of grey hair. We talked disapprovingly about Abiy Ahmed and the Nobel Peace Prize. I tried to hide my competitive side, but the other brooms were shameful specimens, their soft coconut bristles inadequate in the damp. I became irritated when the woman whose trousers appeared to be holding something heavy in the crotch swapped her broom for mine. She didn't even know to loosen her elbow to get a decent sweep. She didn't think to straighten her arm at the end of each push. I watched as my ebullient bristles were dragged pathetically over the tarmac until I could bear it no more. I turned my back on all the detritus escaping on the breeze and wished Violene back from the dead.

Her heavy wool scarf wrapped like a wreath around her head, she'd be out every morning clearing the path. There was nothing that woman couldn't teach you about swigging beetroot punch before breakfast, or how to give unconditional love.

After her extended family took Violene away, Lass invited us round. You were concerned he'd make us drink rum and watch horse racing on the TV, so when I went over and knocked on the door, he was disappointed that I was alone. He poured me whisky and tore into the government and I removed his socks and pruned his fungal toenails.

Later, I discovered dozens of McVitie's Jamaica Ginger Cakes stacked in the cupboard under the sink. He laughed when I said I was searching for jewels. Or cash, I said, nudging him for another smile, but when I looked up he was blinking back tears. Seeing you down there, kneeling on the linoleum, he said, you remind me of my mother. My poor dad, she used to hit him something rotten. Lass tugged the tea towel from the rubber sucker above my head and pressed it to his eyes. Don't ever beat your man, will you? he said, his plea muffled by cloth. We've got to stick together to survive this bitch of a country, I'm totally bloody serious! He stopped shouting and heaved into the despair hanging between us.

It was only when I finally stood up and he led me into the front room that his mood lightened. He encouraged me to choose something I liked. Something that will remind you of me and Violene, he said. He suggested the sofa, insisting we'd be doing him a favour, but I tend to slide off upholstered leather and I get nauseous from the smell.

So I chose, instead, the buxom orange lamp with its enormous hessian shade.

It's so big, there are days when I catch it peering out, watching me, from the corner of the room. The night I brought it home, I knocked the shade while climbing the stairs and damaged its frame. When I set it down on the bedroom floor, to stop it from tipping over I had to prop it up between the old pine cupboard and the wall. This meant it was almost completely out of view, unless you happened to be standing by the window to the right of the old chest. This began to irritate me so much that, shortly before Christmas, I decided to try and get it mended. I wanted to see it standing freely, away from the wall. I wanted it exposed like the rest of us. So I emailed a family-run business in Lancashire that specialises in repairing large lampshades. I attached photographs, including close-ups of all the dents. Five months on they've still not replied.

I'm still not sure of how we learned about Lass's name.

I think it was a Friday morning, the day we all got drunk in the street. I think it was Violene's wake. What I'm certain of is how white and how foolish I felt. This revelation, linking Lass, inextricably in my mind, to the eighteenth-century Yorkshireman, Edwin Lascelles, who followed in his father's footsteps and made a fortune from the forced labour of several thousand enslaved Africans on his sugar plantations in Barbados, Grenada, Jamaica and Tobago.

You said it made you feel as if we had been holding on to the end of a piece of rope that extended over hundreds of years and thousands of miles to something so terrible, something so replete with dread, it was like noticing that the tattoo on your neighbour's arm was a number and, in the sharpened seconds of that moment, catching yourself witnessing the horrors they'd survived.

Now, at night, when the rest of the house is dark and we are lying in bed and you are snoring softly by my side, I observe the lamp. I watch the way the light comes through the shade, thickening to a warm red glow, and how the weave of hessian threads melds with the welts from whips with nine knotted tails. If I look away, if I return to my book or stroke your shoulder and watch the hairs on your arm flutter beneath my breath, every time I raise my gaze and let my eyes loose upon the lamp, the wounds have multiplied, they are all I can see, and I feel astonished that this solid thing that can neither move of its own volition, nor speak to me of misery and despair, can burrow so deeply into my mind that it reaches what must surely be my soul.

The very next morning, when the curtains are open and the blinds rolled up, this same orange lamp, with its vague and crooked shade, behaves as if nothing occurred in the night. As if it is simply a lamp with a job to cast light. As if its torn flesh, bleeding and raw, was a hallucination plucked from a dream – like Jorge, that morning in Marvão, when he stepped through the French windows on to the terrace, his whole body entirely calm.

He wished me good morning and gestured to the sun. He set down a tray of croissants and coffee before hurrying back to the kitchen to fetch the juice he had made with sliced oranges, squeezed, he told me, in his bare hands. I can still hear the cut of his voice, stark as an axe, when he said, on his return, I trust you slept well. I think I responded with a Yes, or a Not bad, or It was quite warm, but not one word about the cupboard I'd pushed against the door, or the thuds I could hear, and the pleading to stop, to please stop, to please leave me alone. I was too afraid. I was trying to work out how I could escape.

When Catarina finally appeared, she was wearing a denim dress that opened on to her shoulders with such elegance I wanted to trace the length of her neck and the angular space beneath her jaw with the nail of my thumb. But my view was interrupted by Jorge, who stood up to greet her, grabbing her fingers and brushing his face against her forehead before reaching into his pocket to pull out the lighter.

He held the short flame to the end of her cigarette, which was jerking and twitching in her trembling hand until he grabbed her wrist in his other fist and fixed it, firm and still.

Things I live with use their stillness to goad me. The glossy white toilet is so resolutely immobile, I've developed the urge to wrench it from the floor and shove it out of place.

For a dozen years I've unbuttoned or unzipped, I've lifted and pulled down. I've spread my pelvis over its gaping jaw, like a spatchcock chicken splayed naked on the grill. I have been comforted upon this solid ceramic to empty my bladder and bowels into its deep, watery bowl. Grateful for the privacy, I was fortunate to be able to stay at home to bleed and groan for the hours it took an embryo to detach and die. This lavatory has let me lie low, engulfing life and swamping death, evacuating all evidence of passion and bad luck.

Slumped upon its plastic lip, I have felt held by this thing that knows me so well. I have felt intimate with this thing that knows you, too. Your dilating arse and hanging cock, your teeth and tongue, and the shaved skin that slackened on your cheeks when you bent over the bowl to purge yourself of my wild stew.

Did I ever tell you about the boy whose family turned its back on Ayatollah Khomeini and came to London to live here instead? He had a nickname that sounded like flossy, which is a lovely word to say softly on one's own. He had a smooth face and gentle eyes, this boy, and the buds of a moustache beginning to show on his upper lip. When he spoke, he punctuated his phrases with sniffs that petered out at the back of his throat.

The room in which we met was fitted with a pale pink carpet that was thick enough to wade through. The walls were covered in wallpaper that was embossed with swirls of apricot velvet. Above the sofa was a large mirror with a heavy gold frame and in front of it, four lion legs supporting a marble slab, which was covered in newspapers and packets of cigarettes, and books that looked like weapons they were so heavy and so hard.

Within a few weeks of arriving in England, this boy was sent to board at one of the oldest and most expensive fee-paying schools in the country. There, a group of fellow pupils frog-marched him into the toilets, forced him into a cubicle and pushed his head down the loo. While several of them held him down, another one pulled the chain.

According to declassified documents, during the 1970s soldiers in the British army used drowning – what we now call waterboarding – as a method of torture in Northern Ireland. On two occasions, one young man

> was forced to lie on his back on the floor, a wet towel had been placed over his head, and water had been poured over it to give him the impression that he would be suffocated; then, when he had got up, he had been required to run the gauntlet of batons wielded by the Army.

Why do I want to be waterboarded? Why am I jealous of Christopher Hitchens, who was asked to subject himself to waterboarding in order to write about the experience for *Vanity Fair*? I got more from watching the video of his ordeal, but he certainly produced a robust and uncomfortable read. Contrary to what the authorities like to tell us – Hitchens calls it the official lie – waterboarding is not simulated drowning. It may be slow, it may be controlled, it may also be halted, but the reason it feels like drowning, Hitchens concluded, is because it is drowning.

Months after the experience, which took place in a secret location in North Carolina, he continued to suffer panic attacks. If I do anything that makes me short of breath, he wrote, I find myself clawing at the air with a horrible sensation of smothering and claustrophobia.

This description, particularly the phrase clawing at the air, only deepens my envy. I want to know, for myself, what it is to be waterboarded. I want to experience that level of panic for life, to notice the dread when the weight of water runs over my hooded face and I try to make myself breathe out, but immediately breathe in, inadvertently sucking the wet towel and mask into my mouth and nostrils, my arms and hands strapped to the sides of my body and my legs tied to the plank upon which I am lying, and someone's fingers pushing down on my solar plexus feeling for the optimal moment to pour on more water. Always, more water.

I want to be forced to consider whether or not I have even a fraction of the insane discipline possessed by Khalid

Sheikh Mohammed, who was named the principal architect of the 9/11 attacks in the *Final Report of the National Commission on Terrorist Attacks Upon the United States.*

Apparently, he held out for two minutes.

Hitchens managed a few seconds.

What could I manage?

For years I've worried that I would surrender to any torturer before the torture had even begun. Certainly, I would be a highly effective member of the resistance, but only to the point of capture. The moment I was confronted with the possibility of extreme pain, I would betray my comrades. I doubt I could manage even a single nail being levered from a toe. I have, nevertheless, taken a few small steps to try to strengthen my tolerance of pain. On the two occasions I have had to have a colonoscopy, for example, I have opted to go without a local anaesthetic. The second time round I didn't even take gas, instead swearing effervescently each time the camera hit another bend.

Do you remember the time we stopped at that petrol station on the east edge of Oxford? You were waiting in the car when I returned with the bag of sandwiches, the eclair toffees, the smoothie and a bunch of bananas, and suddenly felt the sensation of warm liquid flowing into my pants. I hurried back into the shop and into the toilet, where I stuffed a wodge of loo roll into my pants.

Returning to the shop floor, I located a box of Tampax and joined the queue again. I thought I recognised the man standing in front of me and focused carefully when he pulled out his credit card to pay for his petrol. My eyesight was better in those days. I could see the name on the card. It was Peter Hitchens.

He caught my eye when the woman on the till commented on my single item. I would have thought you'd be past that by now, she said.

When I learned about the way those boys bullied that young Iranian lad, I wanted my own head to be held down the loo. And I could, if I wanted, right now, attach a metre of string to the handle of the chain and, whilst kneeling on the ground, push the crown of my head into the mouth of the bend at the back of the bowl, and flush the toilet myself.

I can imagine crouching on a tiled floor splashed with urine, surrounded by teenagers, my head down the loo. I can see faeces and pieces of torn toilet paper getting caught in my eye lashes and trapped in my hair, floating beside my nose and tickling my tongue.

When I imagine being waterboarded, I see a clean, white flannel laid over my face. I see a pale man in a pale blue shirt tucked into pressed chinos. He's wearing surgical gloves and holding a measuring jug full of water.

Is hygiene one of the reasons why waterboarding is an appealing form of torture? Does cleanliness obscure cruelty? Could this explain why the men who tortured my old friend, Fofo, made him lick his own blood off the floor? If they couldn't see the evidence of their violence, could they convince themselves they were doing no real harm?

I've been surprised to learn how many children can't defecate at school. I met one teenager who told me he had never done a poo during the school day. You said he probably had a shy bowel. You are always talking about shy bowels. I'd never heard of them until I met you. You suffered terribly when you travelled across the southern edge of the Sahara. There was nowhere to hide, you said. You can't shit in a tent.

I've always been able to poo wherever and whenever I want. Occasionally I'm overcome with the urge to defecate while out running and I've squatted in many a ditch, among overgrown brambles, clumps of nettles and behind all sorts of bushes that line public playing fields around the country.

Only twice have I felt ashamed about shitting in the open. Once, in a field off the M5. I was with the dog, who swiftly sucked up my slug of dung with such glee I almost threw up. The other time was when I realised that I was shitting beneath a hedge that backed on to a childrens' playground. A single toddler caught sight of me through the leaves. The child stared but said nothing. This should have been cause for relief given the number of adults chatting by the slide. Instead, I felt considerable guilt. Even more, after I told you.

When I examine the toilet from the corner of my eye, its slippery white curves look like the cartilage at the end of a roasted chicken's leg. That's the bit I like to run my tongue over before grinding it down between my back teeth and sucking up the purple marrow, the granular texture thrilling the roof of my mouth.

It's always a surprise, the metallic flavour of cooked blood, and the way you watch me enjoying my bones, your face straining with disgust and pride. I notice your expression and I see you as a boy in honey-brown trousers and a polyester shirt, its long collar points reaching for your ribs. The room fills with sharpened light and the clear notes of that blackbird in the sycamore tree beside the tracks.

Sitting on the loo, I like to place my right elbow on the wooden sill and, using the four fingers of my right hand, bat open the plastic window of the cat flap that was installed at the bottom of the large glass pane. I like the noise it makes as it is released from the magnet and swings out into the open air and then back again, passing through the vertical, defying the magnetised frame, into my waiting fingers and thumb. I like to catch it clean and hold it wide open so I can peer through the rectangular hole.

From up here, I can look down into the garden. I can see the blue tits and the great tits pecking upside down at the fat balls held in the cage that is hanging by a piece of green string from the ceanothus. From up here, I can count the snails crossing the damp grass. I can watch the parking inspector who takes breaks on our side street to call his mother in Kumasi.

Sometimes, when I'm wandering around our neighbourhood looking at people's front doors and their gardens covered in concrete, I'll glance up at the smaller window at the side of a semi – the window with the vent, the window with frosted glass, the window that doesn't open – and wonder who is sitting up there, shitting up there, looking down at me. I wonder if the man across the road ever watches me, the one whose mother gave him one of her home-bred dogs.

When it first arrived, it was so small, he could hold it in one hand. I remarked that it couldn't have been much bigger than one of his knees. It had such a soft coat, it was hard not to imagine it being bred purely for its fur. It was so ugly, I longed to press my face into its belly of black velvet.

It died when it was two. The folds of skin hanging over its nostrils suffocated it in its sleep. I couldn't help but wonder whether our neighbour had pushed the poor little dog's body into his waste disposal unit. Perhaps the pipes that carry litres of our urine and metres of our faeces down into the sewers also carried this unfortunate animal's minced flesh.

When I think about the destination that my shit shares with that of its owner – this man whose hand I would rather not shake, whose voice I would rather not hear – I think about the intimacy of that which has passed through each of our bodies, from lip and tongue to crack or cock and anal verge, and I picture it blending beneath the ground.

It was shortly after I had been sitting on the loo reading *Remnants of Auschwitz* that it occurred to me that I have spent more time looking into the toilet bowl than I have examining the picture that hangs above. It is a painting of a lane in the woods. It is autumn. It is one of Bernie's oils.

Short, fat strokes of orange and the odd swipe of burgundy and vermilion red form the thick carpet of leaves covering the steep bank rising up and away from the road. In the foreground, the trunk of a beech tree leads my gaze to the top half of the picture, which is filled with the leaves on the trees, all sherbert yellow and smudges of a pale apricot that is remarkably similar to the orange mould at the bottom of our shower curtain. It is split, the trunk, like a divided self that will never be free. The roots are large and lumpy. They stop abruptly at the edge of the road as if they've been sliced off with a maul. The surface of the road is a creamy oyster pink. If I could kneel down and rest the side of my face upon its surface, I know I would feel peace.

I hung the painting above the loo because the orange holds itself with such certainty on the canvas, it lends a defiant quality to the mushroom you chose for the bathroom walls. I put the painting there because I wanted to have time with it on my own, to feel it at my back, silently watching over my body and me. Certainly, I didn't expect this nod to vulnerability to prompt me to return to the question, Do I have it in me to handle my excrement to make my mark?

I've been inspired by the men in the Maze, and the women at Armagh too. Surely some of them must have tried to create a particular image or develop a spontaneous pattern while slapping their shit, and the women their blood, onto the walls and the ceilings of their cells. I like to believe I could capture a chaotic thought or a complicated memory so beautifully it would supersede the stench of the paint.

I look at the woods that Bernie painted and I try to fathom her mind. I push my way into the work that I might reach her somewhere inside. I see her crouched over the canvas, her damp, blue eyes tight with concentration, her lips glossed with saliva, her mouth almost ajar. I see the soft white down that covers her cheeks but is only visible within a certain angle of light. She had so much hair, Bernie, but I never thought of her as a witch.

I did sometimes wonder if she was a man. Everything about her seemed to be held up with kirby grips or wrapped in balls of wool.

I think of hard-boiled eggs and beetroot chopped with chives. I see a serving of potato salad and a paper napkin folded into a triangle and curled into a cup. There is a handmade jug full of water from the tap. Everything is cold. The windows are open on both sides of the room. The floorboards are wonky. They are spongy beneath my feet.

After lunch, Villy would do the washing-up in the bathroom and Bernie would take deep breaths and play the grand piano, rocking backwards and forwards so she could reach the pedals with her toes. Before tea, she would lead us down a steep wooden staircase to a thick red curtain that hung from a pole that, long before, had been the handle of a broom. Behind the curtain, the front door was so heavy, she needed both hands to pull it open. I remember following her over gravel into a rolling garden to hunt among the flowers for hidden chocolates wrapped in foil.

I don't remember a potter's wheel. Nor do I remember a shed. The house was narrow and long. It was white with black lines. A large domino lying on its side. The timber that held its structure was sawn from trees felled some five hundred years ago. It was built during the reign of Henry VIII. I am sure I don't know what that means.

I have glimmers of my childhood visits. I never saw the man who lived downstairs. I knew he was in there alone and I knew that Villy had also lived on the ground floor when he, too, arrived from Prague.

In those days, Bernie had a single bed. When Villy moved upstairs, she got a double and, so I seem to recall, was written out of her parents' will.

Long after Bernie died and some time before I met you, I used to visit Villy at his mansion flat on the northwest edge of the heath. We would sit facing one another in a pair of deep green, densely embroidered armchairs. The sash window was vast – it spread the entire width of the room. I liked to let my gaze settle on the midriff of the plane tree while Villy voiced his memories and asked questions about life. One afternoon, in what turned out to be his last summer, he told me about the time he had travelled to the Black Country to attend the funeral of a man he described as a cousin. I think it is time that I share it with you.

I can't remember any of the details he confided about his cousin's life other than that he had never married nor lived with a partner of any sort. Like Villy, he had no children. His siblings were long dead.

He was, said Villy, a quiet man. Now I come to think of it, he was very much like you. He was someone who liked to let in the light, to allow plenty of space into a conversation, plenty of silence, plenty of air. He might mutter a few words to his old cat, then breathe out slowly and deliberately through his nostrils before answering a question or offering a reply. I always felt he was waiting for others to speak, said Villy, as if he wished to gather evidence at leisure, letting your words swirl about a bit in his own mind before coming back with a response, which was often another question of very few words.

The funeral sounded like a glum affair. Only a handful of people attended, all of them old men in long coats. The morning was shaped by heavy cloud, but it was not until the casket was lowered into the grave shortly before teatime, as Villy put it, that the skies opened for rain. He was staring down at the long pine box, wondering if it contained something more sinister than his cousin's body, when he heard the first pellets of water land on the top of his hat. He looked up and his attention was drawn immediately to the man standing on the other side of the grave, staring straight at him. It was his brother.

Villy looked at me. He eased himself forward and stood up from his chair. Brandy, he said by way of announcement, before taking several unsteady steps towards the kitchen, which was a sliver of a room, more like a short corridor that had been squeezed between the bathroom and an even narrower space he referred to as the library.

I watched him pouring cognac into a pair of teacups while I tried to remember if he'd ever told me about a brother before. I knew he had a small circle of friends from his teaching days and, of course, I knew about his curious relationship with Bernie. Otherwise, I'd always thought of him as a man without family. I'd long assumed he was the only one to survive.

For the rest of the burial, Villy gazed into his cousin's grave. I couldn't bear to look at this man standing in front of me, he said. He took nearly everything! Just a note on the mantelpiece bidding us farewell. Days later, Villy continued, we found out through an acquaintance of his that he'd exchanged our belongings and the little money my parents had left for a train ticket out of Prague.

It was 1938. It was the end of the summer. Villy never spoke to his brother again.

At Villy's funeral the following year, which was the year before I met you, I met a man who told me he'd designed a hydrogen plane. After the service in Middlesex, he gave me a lift to Villy's flat. He said he didn't recognise anyone either. For all I know, he said, prodding me with his elbow, they're a bunch of strangers from the laundry-ette. He repeated the word laundry-ette. I think it tickled him to see me laugh.

The front door was open when we arrived. There were plates of sandwiches and fairy cakes on top of the bookshelves. Small bowls of crisps and peanuts and pieces of cheese stabbed with toothpicks decorated the windowsills and the mantelpiece in the sitting room. Someone had put some gherkins in an avocado dish and left them on the lid of the piano beside a small vase of flowers. On the short wooden shelf at the very end of the keyboard, an abandoned cigarette was burning on one of Bernie's plates.

I found more smokers in the garden. A man, who said he was a mathematician, and a woman, who introduced herself as one of Villy's philosophers, were arguing about Kant. Villy had been writing a book about Popper when he died. I tried to remember the detail of the last conversation we'd had, but all I could see was Villy, cross-legged in his chair, chuckling at something I had said.

Still, I took more of his belongings home than anyone else. I chose a tall pine bookshelf and a painting by Bernie of the sea. I filled a cardboard box with books about spectres and spirits and mourning and the mind, about torture and pain and debt. One I chose because of the dark monochrome photograph on the cover. It is the head of a man without any hair. You see the shape of his skull beneath the cloak of his skin. Curious white scratch marks appear to float just above his face, as if the photographic film was once covered in clay or painted or buried in the ground. It is unnerving that this stark portrait reminds me strongly of you. I doubt I'll ever be able to disentangle the shadows that appear on your face in the wintry light of our room from those of the man who survived the Third Reich.

After much encouragement from the woman who cleaned Villy's flat for all those years – she inherited his tortoise as well as most of his estate – I filled a second cardboard box with what remained of Bernie's ceramics. I don't know why we don't use the espresso cups more often. I seem to be happy just knowing they are there, safe, on the top shelf. Sometimes, I open the cupboard door simply to look at them. Occasionally, I bring them down and line them up as if preparing for a gathering of porcelain dolls.

My favourite is the one that's missing a saucer. Its glaze is Nanking blue washed with a warm pinkish grey, a pale green and the odd touch of brown. When you asked me to describe it in one word I said thunder. On further reflection I thought Turner and felt a sudden rush to ask you if you had ever seen the painting *Slavers Throwing Overboard the Dead and the Dying*, but something stopped me, I'm not sure what. I think I was overwhelmed with self-doubt. Then that haunting sentence came to mind. The one I read online, or was it somewhere in a book? The Black is essentially a human refashioned into a thing and forced to endure the fate of an object or a tool. With this cascade of history tearing through me, I heard you say Morandi, then the ocean sea. Next, you muttered something about a bolt for a large hole, but I didn't understand what you meant.

I told you that the handle was too small for the cup. I described it as being deformed. I said, I wish I knew why Bernie had given it thalidomide. I hoped you would respond but your expression remained blank. The stillness of your face confounded me for days.

After you moved out of your bedsit and moved in with me, I showed you Bernie's tiny salt pot with its perfect little lid. I served you gooseberry fool in one of the goblets. You asked to see the two platters that, according to Villy, Bernie had painted with rows of mussels to try to take her mind off the Cuban missile crisis. You admired the cake stand most of all, and we've used it every birthday ever since. You said you wished you'd met her before she died. You said it was obvious she had designed the smaller, square plates with toast in mind. You said, Spreading butter onto a slice of hot thick white on one of these is ceremonial. You laughed with so much pleasure I wondered if you were really laughing about something else.

What I like about the square plates is the lift of the lip around the edge. Just high enough to keep the crumbs on board. And I have noticed, when you are using one of these plates, that you hold your knife with the tips of your fingers, not rammed into your fist, which is what you do when you eat off one of those large dinner plates you bought at the charity shop in Crewe while we were waiting for the rail replacement bus to take us to your uncle's funeral at Morecambe Bay. They've got to be the ugliest plates I've ever seen, but you like them because of their size. Big enough for two helpings, unlike Bernie's, which are fragile and small and prompt a delicacy of touch.

I don't think you've noticed that I've stopped eating off the blue one. It's because of what I saw in the paint. Four melancholy figures. Their hands are clasped and they are in the rain. They are looking at something we cannot see, something beyond the edge of the plate. I think I forgot I had broken it, until you told me to close my eyes and you took my fingers in yours and you rubbed them over the surface, where you had glued it, imperceptibly, back together, and I told you about the blue canvas blind in my childhood bedroom.

I must have been six or seven when I stood naked on the wooden sill, trying to reach the piece of cord, to pull it down so I could go to bed. A man was walking past on the pavement below. He looked up and saw this pale, slender child, her skin as tight as a whippet's. She was pointing her toes and wriggling her hips. Her fingers scratched at the glass pane.

When I realised it was your old camera tripod abandoned among the Portuguese laurels at the side of the road, I was overcome with regret. This awkward ally, all legs and long neck, had accompanied you almost everywhere since you and I first met. It might as well have been me standing there, on the verge, soaking wet. Staring, from across the road, my eyes so familiar with this tall, sinister shape, the grief felt overwhelming. How could you be so cruel?

I thought of Villy and what he had told me about the day his brother upped and left. His father unlocked the front door and Villy and his mother walked into the hallway, which was usually cramped because of the old coat stand in front of the mirror, but neither stand nor mirror were there any more. The three of them walked into the sitting room. The beautiful octagonal table with its scalloped pedestal leg, at which Villy and his brother had done their homework together every night for years, had gone. His mother's deep green sewing machine, also gone. The brass tongs and the log poker, the coal scuttle with cosmos flowers carved into the lid, the serving trolley, the brass candlestick, all gone. His grandmother's steamer trunk, which had always stood on its end by the window with a large-leafed house plant on top, had also gone. His father's typewriter. The dining table and its six chairs. The silver vase that occasionally held a single flower, and the silver cutlery his parents were given on their wedding day. The leather frames that had held photographs of his four grandparents. The rocking chair with embossed leather upholstery, which, his father liked to boast, came from Austria, had also gone. His father's writing desk. His mother's leather handbag. Her entire jewellery collection inside its leather case. The carriage clock that had been passed down to his mother from her great aunt. The wireless that his father had screwed to the wooden ledge in the hatch between the kitchen and the dining room. All the rugs. His father's Junghans clock. Even the gold-nibbed Ripet fountain pen, given to Villy by his uncle Peter before he, too, had fled Prague a few months prior.

And yet, said Villy, despite my mother's tears and my father's despair, it was less the absence of all these things that terrified me than the sound their disappearance left behind.

Now, the house was breathing, he said. Now, the house was alive.

Thank you to the Society of Authors for awarding me an Authors' Foundation Grant. Thank you to the following editors for publishing extracts from the book: to Vlatka Horvat and Tim Etchells for including 'Because Everything In This Damned World' in *Seen from Here: Writing in the Lockdown* (Unstable Objects, 2020); to Diane Williams and the wonderful team at NOON for publishing 'Lucky Charm' in *NOON The Literary Annual*, 2021; and to Wendy Erskine for including the short extract, 'Spent Light', in *well I just kind of like it* (PVA Books, 2022).